COPY 19 ✔

Tales from Atop a Russian Stove

TALES
FROM ATOP
A RUSSIAN STOVE

by Janet Higonnet-Schnopper

Illustrated by Franz Altschuler

ALBERT WHITMAN & Company, Chicago

1 - 3 - 74
c. 19

Library of Congress Cataloging in Publication Data

Higonnet-Schnopper, Janet, comp.
    Tales from atop a Russian stove.

    CONTENTS: pt. 1: Of craft and cunning. The
soldier's fur coat.—If you don't like it, don't
listen.—Who'll wash the porridge pot?—Anfy and
his landlord. [etc.]
    1. Tales, Russian. [1. Folklore—Russia]
I. Title
PZ8.1.H538Tal   398.2'0947   70-188430
ISBN 0-8075-7755-3

Contents

Introduction

To all children in the three and seventh, three eleventh kingdom —

That's how the Russian story begins. But close your eyes for a minute. Along the wall of the room imagine a big box, twice as high as your own bed and twice as wide. The box is built of brick and clay and is warm because a gentle fire is burning inside. What can it be? That big clay box is a Russian stove!

The stove is large enough to sit on, even large enough to sleep on. It has doors in the side for baking and keeping food warm — just like your mother's oven. But the Russian stove is much more than a place to cook: the top of the stove is where the story-teller sits.

Russian children, and adults too, have always gathered together around the stove to hear the old tales of their land. Some of the stories have been told for hundreds of years and are still being told right this minute in Russia. Of course the stories may grow and change a little, because the storyteller uses whatever he remembers or adds whatever new adventures he imagines.

But no matter what he chooses to say, the storyteller makes the adventures come alive again. The bear comes out of his burrow and teases the silly fox, the firebird shoots across the sky looking for the golden apple tree, and great Russian warriors ride again across the steppe clanking their spurs and swords and looking for an enemy invader or a roaring dragon.

The stories in this book have been translated from the Russian and adapted for reading in English. The mock heroic language in some of the tales is found in the Russian, while the broad humor and peasant craftiness are also part of the Russian storyteller's bag of tricks. Where verse is traditionally used in the Russian original, it has been kept in the English translation. The folk tales in this collection are found in *Russkie narodnye skazki,* compiled by N. Savushkina, published in 1965 in Moscow.

Pronouncing Russian Names

Russian names look hard to say, but they're not too difficult when you get used to them.

Here is a list of Russian words found in this book with the names spelled in a way that will make them easier to pronounce. Try saying the names aloud when you feel like it. The syllable spelled in capital letters is the accented or stressed part of the word.

You won't need to pronounce the words for reading to yourself, but you might want to tell these stories to your younger brothers and sisters, just as a real Russian storyteller would. Remember, every time you name one of the Russian heroes, an acorn falls off the oak tree behind the house of Baba Yaga the witch. Then it drops down the chimney and hits her on her bony nose!

People

Afonka	ah-PHONE-ka
Alyosha Popovich	ahl-YO-sha pop-O-vitch
Anfy	AN-fee
Apraksia	ah-PRAK-sya
Baba Yaga	BAA-baa yaa-GAA
Bova	BO-va
boyar	boy-AR
Churila Plenkovich	chur-EEL-ah plen-KOV-itch
Efrosina	yeh-fro-SEEN-ah
Eruslan Lazarevich	yeh-roos-LAN laz-ah-RAY-vitch
Foma	fom-AH
Ivan Timofeevich	ee-VAAN tee-mo-FAY-ev-itch
Ivan Tsarevich	ee-VAAN tsa-RAY-vitch
Khan	KAAN
Leonty	lay-OHN-tee
Luba	LOO-ba
Maryshko Paranov	mar-EESH-ko pa-RAAN-of
Mikulisha Selyanin	me-koo-LEESH-ah sell-YAN-in
Mikulov	me-KOOL-of
Nastya	NAAST-ya

Stavr Rodionovich	STAVR
	rod-ee-OHN-o-vitch
Tanya	TAAN-ya
Tsar	TSAAR
Vasilisa	vah-see-LEE-sah
Vasilly	vah-SEE-lee
Vladimir	vlah-DEE-meer
Zabava	zah-BAH-vah

Animal Characters

Katafat Ivanovich	KAT-a-fat
	ee-VAAN-ov-itch
Levon	LYEH-von
Lizaveta Ivanovna	lee-zah-VEH-tah
	ee-VAAN-ov-nah
Mikhailo (Misha)	me-HIGH-low
	(MEE-shah)
Tugarin	too-GAR-in
Zilant	zee-LANT

Places

Chernigov	chair-NEE-gof
Kiev	KEE-ef
steppe	STEP

Part One:
Of Craft and Cunning

The Soldier's Fur Coat

ONCE THERE LIVED AN OLD PEASANT AND HIS WIFE. They weren't bad people, but they were terribly selfish. They would never share anything with a friend or a stranger.

If they were going to market they wouldn't let anyone have a ride in their cart.

"The horse is too tired," they would say, or, "The wheels are old — the wood might split."

If someone wanted to borrow an axe they would sometimes lend it out but not without payment.

"Take the axe," the old man would say, "but we get a bundle of logs for every two bundles you chop."

And the old couple never invited their neighbors to share a good meal, not even at holiday time.

One winter afternoon a soldier passed through the village. He was on his way home after serving in the army.

The soldier had walked a long way. His clothes were ragged and almost worn out. When he reached the village it was time to stop for the night.

He looked in the window of the peasant's hut and saw the old man and his wife inside. The soldier saw a pot bubbling on the stove and smelled a chicken cooking. So he knocked at the door and asked, "Please let me stay here for just one night."

"All right, young man, you can spend the night," said the selfish old man. "But there's nothing for supper except porridge. And in return for dinner and lodging, you must go out after supper and tend the pigs."

The soldier agreed and went inside. The wife was standing by the stove, but there was no sign of the chicken except for the delicious smell inside the hut.

The wife gave the young soldier nothing but a dish of cold porridge to eat. Then she and her husband sent the soldier outside to tend the pigs.

The wife filled two bowls with good chicken soup, and the couple sat down to their own supper.

As the soldier went out to the pig yard, he thought to himself, "I'll just find out what happened to that chicken." He lifted the latch on the gate and let the pigs out.

Then the young man rushed back into the hut

shouting, "Quick! The pigs are loose. They're escaping into the woods!"

The peasant and his wife jumped right up and rushed out of the hut. The soldier stayed behind.

He looked into the bowls where the peasant and his wife had been eating and saw they were still half-filled with good soup. Then he looked behind the stove. Sure enough! There was the cooked chicken in a pot hidden away in the corner.

"Someone ought to play a trick on this selfish pair," the young man thought.

When the peasant and his wife had returned the pigs to the yard it was getting dark.

The winter nights were already very cold. A few flakes of snow began to swirl in the wind.

"Well, you'd better climb up on the stove to sleep, soldier," said the peasant. "It's a cold night."

"What for?" said the soldier. "I have this warm soldier's coat. I'll sleep on the floor."

The young man took his coat and spread it out. He lay down and folded it over him. The coat was large, but it was worn, and it even had a hole or two. The peasant and his wife climbed up on the stove where it was warm.

After a while it grew very dark. The wind blew harder and shook the rickety door of the hut. Little showers of snow came in through the cracks.

But the soldier said to the peasant, "Could you please make the fire die down a little? It's very warm here."

The peasant and his wife were surprised. They were nice and cozy on the stove, but they knew how cold it must be on the floor of the hut. But they shut the door of the stove as the soldier had asked.

A little later the soldier spoke up again. "Could you please open the door of the hut? It's stuffy and I can't breathe."

"I can't do that," answered the peasant. "We'll all freeze."

The wife whispered to her husband, "In the morning, go have a little talk with the soldier about his coat. That ragged coat doesn't look like much, but it must be warm. Ask him whether he won't exchange it for a new fur coat. With the fur coat that's here we could never sleep on the floor and be warm like that."

In the morning they all got up.

The soldier said, "Ekh! I'm nearly dead, sleeping on the floor wrapped in my coat. It was so hot I couldn't stand it."

The peasant said to the soldier, "Why don't you exchange that coat of yours for this new fur we have here? Your coat is too warm for you. But I have to go out to chop wood and do business at the market.

The fur coat is a bit on the heavy side for working.
Make an exchange."

The soldier hesitated.

"Go ahead," said the wife. "We'll add a little
payment on the side."

The young man thought another minute.
Finally he said, "Well, all right, just for you. You
people were so kind to let me spend the night here
and to give me supper. Take the coat."

So the soldier put on the peasant's fur coat and
was on his way.

He smiled to himself as he thought how well
he had gotten even with the selfish old peasant and
his wife. Now he was nice and warm in his new coat.
He walked happily, heading for home.

The old peasant, bundled in the soldier's coat,
climbed into his cart to go to the market.

The wind blew and the snow came in through
the ragged places. The frost got colder and colder.
The peasant's teeth chattered. He could hardly move
his lips. When he got to the market he was so cold
he had to turn right around and come home. And
on the way home he had to give some other poor
fellow a ride just to have another warm person next
to him in the cart. Otherwise he would have been
frozen through and through.

So much for selfishness!

If You Don't Like It, Don't Listen

ONCE THERE LIVED — THERE REALLY DID — AN OLD woman and an old man. They had a son named Ivan.

The family lived well enough on not too much and not too little. Then the old man died. The woman and her son were very poor after that. But the years passed and the son grew up.

One day Ivan needed to go to the market, so he asked his mother whether she had any errands for him.

She had just finished spinning two skeins of wool, so she said, "Take my wool to the market and sell it for me."

"I'll do it," said Ivan. Then he told her his plans in a little rhyme:

> "I'll bring the wool to market—
> Two bags full.

Ivan knows how to bargain
And sell your wool.
But if my purse stays empty—
No sign of wealth!—
I'll tap a few full pockets
And help myself.''

"What are you saying, child?" Ivan's mother exclaimed. "That isn't right!"

"Why go right?" asked Ivan. "If left is right and right is left, then the right way is the wrong way."

He put the skeins of wool in a bag, grabbed his hat, and went to the market.

At the market Ivan sold the wool for ten rubles and got ninety more by his clever tricks. So all in all, he ended up with a hundred rubles. That was a lot of money to jingle in his pocket.

He bought a stack of honey cakes and some honey beer and set off for home in the cart.

The cart jolted along, stopping now and then for a crossroad or a deep hole. But Ivan never stopped eating.

He sat cross-legged on the cart, tossing cakes from the heap in front of him into the air and catching them in his mouth.

Up went a cake, and chomp! down into his throat. Then he would tip back his head and take a gulp of beer.

As he was going along like that, Ivan happened to meet up with a noble gentleman.

The nobleman was galloping along the road in a carriage pulled by not just one but four horses. He forced everything on the road out of the way and into the mud.

Out of the corner of his eye Ivan saw the carriage coming. "Why should I make way for him?" the young man thought. "There must be a way to stop him."

The nobleman's horses snorted and pranced and tried to rush past Ivan's old cart. When the nobleman's carriage drew near, Ivan tossed up a honey cake and it flew right into the nobleman's lap!

Ivan didn't pull off the road into the ditch, so the nobleman couldn't get by. The gentleman was indignant.

"Hey there, little fellow! What do you think you're doing! Since when does a peasant toss around honey cakes? You'd think the cakes alone would do— but just look at that! You're gulping down beer like a merchant on Saturday night!"

"Why shouldn't I eat well?" Ivan answered. "I just went to the market and I earned ten rubles for my mother's wool and ninety for my own cleverness. I could get at least two hundred from you."

"You could, could you?" cried the nobleman.

"All right then, if you're so clever, just use your wits on me!"

Ivan stopped eating and made an elaborate bow.

"In that case, noble sir, be so kind as to make a bet with me. If you say to me 'You're lying!' while I tell you a story, you lose two hundred rubles. But if you can keep from saying it, then you get my hundred and you can do what you want with me. I'll even go down in the ditch and get out of your way."

"Agreed!" cried the nobleman. "That's easy! But watch out! I'll be thinking all the while of what I'll do with you when I win."

So they shook hands on it and Ivan began telling tall tales.

"When I was just a little boy, still in the cradle at my mother's and father's—they both had big black beards—I went off one day for a walk in the woods. It was spring, and all the leaves had turned red and yellow.

"In the woods I saw a tree, and in the tree was a hole. In the hole some roasted quail had woven a nest. So I stuck one arm into the hole, but I couldn't reach the nest. Then I stuck in a leg, but I still couldn't reach it. So I bent down and jumped in, hup! I flew in all at once. Then I sat down at the table and had a fine dinner. I ate as much as I

wanted, meat, bones, and all. The quails sang a little song for me when I finished them off.

"Then I decided to crawl out again. But that was hopeless. I'd gotten all puffed out and fat from so much eating, and my legs had gotten shorter. The hole was getting smaller all the time. But, like a clever fellow, I figured out how to escape. I ran off home to get an axe. Then I chopped the wood around the edges of the hole, and climbed out."

"True enough," murmured the nobleman. "It's all true."

"Then," Ivan continued, "I felt a great urge to drink something after my dinner, so I went down to the sea. I took off my head and used it for a cup and started drinking. I had drunk just about enough and everything seemed to be fine when—whoops!—I dropped my head into the water. I looked around everywhere and finally saw it floating in the middle of the sea. Some ducks and geese had made their nests in it and had laid eggs.

"What could I do? I took out my axe and threw it at the nest. The first throw fell short, the second try went too far, and on the third, the axe went up into the air and didn't come down again. And that's how I knocked all the ducks and geese out of my head. The eggs just flew away on their own.

"After that, I went to the edge of the sea, rolled

it up, and set it on fire. When the sea was burned up
I got my head back and went out to take a tour
around the wide world."

"Just keep at it, little fellow," said the nobleman. "Just keep talking. Everything you say is as
true as true can be."

"Then I went into the woods for kindling wood.
While I was wandering around and cutting wood,
a pack of blue wolves ran up and tore open my
horse's belly. But I was clever enough for that. I
hacked off a birch branch and came running to the
horse. I gathered up all the pieces of the horse, put
them back inside, and sewed up the horse with the
birch branch. I filled my cart with what was left over
and got ready to go. I shook the reins, but the horse
didn't budge.

"'What's going on here?' I thought. So I looked
up and saw that the birch branch had grown up into
a tall tree, the tallest tree you could find. The pine
needles at the top poked right up through the clouds.
So I decided to climb up into Heaven. I looked
around up there and gave everything the once-over.

"Soon the clock in my pocket was striking
thirteen. It was time to go back down. But I had
more bad luck to come. My horse had moved off
and knocked down the willow. What could I do?
How could I get back to earth?

"I started gathering dust and dead leaves up there and wove myself a rope. I tied that rope to a cloud, and soon I was heading downward. I slid down, down, as long as the rope held out. But when I got to the end of the rope I had to think up something else. So I cut some rope off up above and added it on below, and I slid down a little more. Then I cut some more rope off above, added it on below, and slid farther, and so on down, cutting above and adding below.

"But I finally got to where there was nothing more to cut off, and it was still a long way to earth! Then, to top it off, a strong wind came up and started rocking me back and forth, knocking me in all directions. The rope broke, and where did I fall? Not just to earth, but way down into the very depths, to a place it isn't easy to get out of. Yes, noble sir, I wasn't on earth any more at all, but down in Hell! There I saw your own father harnessed to a cart and pulling manure around for the devil's garden and—"

"What? You fool! You're lying!" burst out the nobleman.

Well, that was that. A bet is a bet. Ivan collected his money from the noble gentleman and drove off again, heading for home. His mother was glad to see him. He showed her the money for the wool and the bet. She called in guests and relatives for a celebration when she saw how their fortunes had changed. They set up tables and had a party.

. . .

"I shared their cheer and drank honey beer.
I was covered with froth but dry in the mouth.
They gave me a cap and started to clap.
And so, my dear friend, has the story an end—
But drinking of beer goes on till the morning!"

Who'll Wash the Porridge Pot?

ONCE THERE LIVED — MAYBE YOU ALREADY KNOW about it — a very old man and his old wife. They were poor, so they didn't live very well. And they were very lazy, too. Neither one of them ever wanted to do any work.

The man would get up in the morning and put his shoes on. But he was too lazy even to tie the laces. When he went outside, his shoelaces would catch on something, and he would start grumbling.

"What are you grumbling about?" his wife would ask from inside the hut.

"It's these laces," the old man would answer. "I can't figure out what to do about them. They keep getting in my way."

Then, standing there, he would stare at the laces for a while. Then he would sit down to keep from tripping on them. So no work would get done.

When it was time for supper, the man would

say to his wife, "It's time for some tea. Get some water and put the kettle on."

The old woman would take down the bucket and go to the well. She would lower the bucket into the well. But when the bucket was full of water and heavy, she was too lazy to draw it up again. She would lean over the edge of the well, look down at the bucket, and sigh. Then she would go back to the hut.

"You can't get any water from that well," she would say to her husband.

So they didn't live very well.

Once the old woman made a pot of porridge. It was good porridge and the two of them ate almost all of it. But a little was still left sticking to the inside of the pot. At first the porridge was just sticky; then it got hard.

The husband and his wife sat at the table. Neither one wanted to wash the pot.

The old man said, "Wash the pot, wife."

"No, you wash it," she answered.

The old man grumbled. The old woman sighed. Neither one washed the pot. "Well, all right, then," they said to each other. "Don't wash the pot."

They both went to bed and there the pot stood, unwashed.

The old man and his wife lay in bed for a while and then they made an agreement.

"Tomorrow morning," said the old man, "the first one who says a word washes the pot."

"All right," said the old woman.

They slept through the night. Then it was morning. They both went on lying there in bed.

The old man didn't say a word. The old woman didn't either.

The two of them were still lying in their bed when it was nearly noon. When nothing stirred around the hut, the village people began to notice it. They started to gather around. Then the villagers went inside to see what was wrong.

About five people were there. The old man and the old woman were still lying in their bed, not saying a word.

The neighbors came over and asked, "What's the matter with you two?"

But the old man and his wife kept silent.

Before long, the people of the village had all gathered. The hut and the yard were filled with townsfolk. The people talked to the man and his wife, banged on the stove, and even shouted. But neither the man nor his wife said a word.

"What can we do now?" the townspeople asked.

"Better send for the priest," someone said.

"Maybe he'll know what's the matter with them," another person said.

So they sent for the priest and stood there waiting for him to come.

The priest arrived at the hut, went right inside, and asked the old couple, "What's happened here? You must tell us."

The old man and his wife were wide awake. But they didn't answer. The priest couldn't get a word out of them no matter how hard he tried.

"The devil has something to do with this," said the priest. "Something has happened here and we can't just leave them alone. Someone has to stay here and keep an eye on them."

One of the village women said, "Well, I can stay, I guess, and keep an eye out. But I ought to be paid for it. What do I get for staying and taking care of them?"

The priest looked around the hut and saw the old woman's new Sunday clothes hanging on a hook. "There's a dress hanging up over there," he said. "It looks new. You can take it in return for your services."

When the old woman heard that, she jumped up off the bed. "What!" she cried. "You think I'd give up my new dress? Well, I won't!"

"Ha!" the old man cried, sitting up in bed. "Now you have to wash the pot."

And wash it the old woman did.

Anfy and His Landlord

IN THE THREE AND SEVENTH, THREE ELEVENTH KING-
dom there lived a landlord. He had plenty of money.

One day this landlord went to the market and
bought a canary for his wife. The canary had yellow
feathers and could sing. He paid fifty rubles for it.

A peasant named Anfy was standing nearby
when the landlord bought the canary. Anfy went
home and said to his wife Marya, "You know what,
Marya?"

"What?" the woman asked.

"I was at the market today," Anfy said, "and our
landlord was there, too. He bought a tiny yellow
bird, not big at all. And he paid fifty rubles for it!
Why don't I just bring him our goose? He likes birds
so much, maybe he will buy it."

"Take it and see," said Marya.

So the peasant took the goose and brought it to the landlord.

"Buy this goose," Anfy said.

"How much?" asked the landlord.

"A hundred rubles."

"You're crazy!" said the landlord. He took a puff on his pipe and laughed at Anfy. "That's just a plain goose."

"You're the one who's a fool," answered Anfy. "You didn't mind paying fifty rubles for a tiny yellow bird. A hundred rubles should be cheap for this fat one."

The goose honked and wiggled its tail.

Anfy's disrespect made the landlord angry. He gave Anfy a knock on the head, took the goose, and slammed the door without paying the peasant anything at all.

"All right," said Anfy. "You won't forget that goose of mine!"

Then he went back home. He sat down at the table, put his head in his hands, and sat there thinking. He sat at the table all morning. Then he sat some more, still thinking.

When Marya began rattling her pots and pans, Anfy got up from the table, tugged at his beard, and paced the floor. Then he sat right down again to eat his dinner. He had finally thought of a way to get even with the landlord.

One day about a month later, when the landlord had forgotten all about how he had acted, Anfy
got up early and said to his wife, "Tomorrow the
landlord will come to collect his rent. Boil thirty
eggs and I'll take them to sell at the market."

It was almost Easter, and the price of eggs was
high. When the eggs were boiled, Marya and Anfy
painted them red and yellow. Then Anfy went to
the market to sell them. He got one ruble for each
egg, so he had thirty rubles.

But Anfy didn't take the rent money home.
Instead, he went into the tavern near the marketplace, gave the owner ten rubles, and said, "I'll be
back tomorrow. Don't forget that you owe me ten
rubles' worth of food and drink."

Then Anfy went to another tavern on the other
side of town. Here, too, he gave the tavernkeeper ten
rubles and said, "Tomorrow I'll come back. I'll order
ten rubles' worth to eat and drink. But don't forget
that I've already paid."

Then Anfy went into a third tavern and made
the same arrangement. After that he went back home.

When he reached his home, Anfy went out into
the field and caught two big black crows. He put
one in a cage and one in a closet inside the house.
Then he went out to the barn and brought in empty

sacks, an old plough, a broken wheel, and some sticks of wood. He laid all these things in the middle of the floor.

Then Anfy said to Marya, "Tomorrow morning the landlord will come here to collect his rent. Let him in the house. Then tell him I am at the market getting money to pay what I owe him. He can find me in the marketplace tavern. When the landlord leaves, you clean up all these things I just dragged into the house. Then get a nice dinner ready. And let that other crow out of the closet. Don't forget about that crow! It's very important. I will take the first crow with me."

Marya knew Anfy had something clever up his sleeve and promised to do everything he asked.

Sure enough, the next morning the landlord came to see Anfy about the rent.

"Come in, sir," said Marya. "Anfy has gone to the market to sell grain and get the money to pay you. You will find him at the marketplace tavern."

"What a lot of things you keep in the house," said the landowner, looking around at the littered floor. He soon left, glad to see no more of that mess.

The landlord found Anfy in the tavern, just as Marya had said. He was sitting at a table with a glass of vodka and good things to eat spread out before him. On one chair stood a cage with a big crow in it.

An old-fashioned four-cornered hat hung from the back of the chair.

"Hello, Anfy," said the landlord. "I've come for the rent."

"Yes, sir," answered Anfy, "here it is, right here. I am sorry to make you come to the market for your rent, but I had to come here myself to get the money. You would honor me by having a glass of vodka and sharing this food."

So Anfy and the landlord sat there together eating and drinking.

When they were finished, Anfy said, "Let's try the tavern over on the other side of town."

"All right," agreed the landowner, glad for the chance to sit and enjoy himself.

Anfy carefully took his hat off the chair. It must have belonged to Anfy's father in the days when he was in the army, the landowner thought.

Anfy called the tavernkeeper over and said, "We've had enough." Then he began to tap with the four-cornered hat on the table.

The tavernkeeper looked at the hat. Anfy tapped with it again. Then Anfy asked, "And what do we owe you?" He still tapped the hat on the table.

"Nothing," answered the tavernkeeper. "Nothing at all."

"In that case," Anfy said, putting on the hat,

"we'll be on our way. Good day to you."

The landlord was surprised that Anfy did not have to pay for the vodka and food. But he did not say anything and followed the peasant to the tavern on the other side of town. Anfy led the way, holding the birdcage.

At the second tavern, Anfy ordered more food and vodka. The landlord shared it with him.

When the men were finished, Anfy took up his hat again and called the tavernkeeper over. He began to tap the hat on the table and asked, "What do we owe you?"

The tavernkeeper stared at the strange, four-cornered hat and then answered, "Nothing. You owe me nothing."

So the two men left the second tavern without laying down even a kopeck.

The landlord began to grow curious about Anfy's hat. Unexplained things seemed to happen when Anfy tapped it on the table. Why hadn't the peasant had to pay anything for all the food and drink in the taverns?

By the time Anfy and the landlord had left the third tavern, the landlord felt he had figured everything out.

In that tavern, just as in the others, Anfy had ordered food and drink and then tapped with his hat when it was time to pay the bill. The secret must be in the hat! The tapping made the innkeepers forget all about how much money Anfy owed.

To himself the landlord said, "There's something special about that hat, that's sure enough. It doesn't even look like a regular peasant's cap. I could use a hat like that. Getting drinks at the tavern for nothing is better than collecting rents."

Aloud he said, "Sell me your hat, Anfy."

"I don't know," said Anfy. "It doesn't look like much. But it's a valuable hat to me."

"Well, I can see that," said the landlord. "But sell it anyway. I will pay you fifty rubles for it and I'll forget about the rent you owe me for a year."

"Well," said the peasant, looking the hat over again, "all right. I'll sell you the hat."

Then Anfy picked up the cage with the crow and started to walk away.

"Wait a minute," called the landlord. "What are you going to do with that old crow you've been carrying around with you?"

"I'm going to sell it," answered Anfy.

"Sell it!" exclaimed the landlord. "Who would want an ordinary crow?"

"Well, now, maybe this bird isn't ordinary," said Anfy. "Come home with me and I'll show you."

"I don't want to go there," said the landowner.

"Your place is a mess. I stopped by there a little while ago."

"That's where the crow comes in," said Anfy. "I'll just send him on home ahead of us with a message. The crow will tell my wife to get things ready."

"No crow can do that," objected the landlord. "Crows can't talk. They don't even sing."

But Anfy went ahead and took the crow out of the cage. He set the bird on his hand and said to it, "Fly home now, crow. Tell Marya, your mistress, to clean up everything in the hut. And tell her to get my dinner ready, too."

Then Anfy let the crow fly from his hand. The bird flew high over the town and out of sight.

"Of course it's impossible for that crow to carry a message," said the landlord. "But maybe I'll just walk by your place and look in." So the landlord went back with Anfy to his house.

When the men walked in the door, the hut was all neat and clean! The sacks, sticks, and broken wheel were gone. The peasant's dinner was waiting on the table. And a black crow was flying around the room.

"Amazing!" exclaimed the landlord. "I've never seen anything like it! Sell me the bird. How much do you want for him?"

"Well, I don't know," said Anfy. "He's very

valuable, but I suppose I could train another one. What do you think, Marya? Should we let him go for fifty rubles?"

"Whatever you think," said Marya.

So the landlord paid out fifty rubles and took the bird from Anfy as well as the four-cornered hat.

On his way home, the landlord decided to stop at one of the taverns, just to try out his new hat. He sat down and ordered a glass of vodka and some salted cucumbers.

When he was finished, he called the tavern-keeper over.

"I've had enough now," the landlord said, taking the four-cornered hat and tapping it on the table. "What do I owe you?"

"A ruble and forty kopecks," said the tavern-keeper.

"What are you saying, my good man?" said the landlord. He tapped faster and harder with the hat.

"Ninety kopecks for the vodka and fifty for the cucumbers. That makes one ruble, forty," answered the tavernkeeper. Then he asked, "What are you tapping your hat for? You'll spoil the corners."

The landlord had to pay the bill. He couldn't understand what had gone wrong.

Maybe, he thought, he hadn't started the tapping soon enough. So he tried the four-cornered hat in another tavern and then another. But he always had to pay the bill! He spent more than five rubles.

Finally the landowner was ready to go home. But he had walked so much and had so many treats at the taverns that he was tired.

Suddenly he remembered his messenger crow. "I'll just send the bird ahead to call for a carriage," he thought.

He took the bird out of the cage and said to it, "Crow, fly away to the manor house by the pine woods. Tell Foma, the coachman, to send a carriage to the marketplace to pick his master up."

Then he tossed the bird into the air and sat down to wait. He waited and waited, but the carriage did not come.

Soon the market stalls closed and the street grew quiet. But the carriage still hadn't come. The landlord was so tired he was ready to fall asleep right there.

He had plenty of time to think over the day and its happenings. "That Anfy," he said at last. "He outsmarted me."

And at home, Anfy just smiled to himself and Marya.

The Clever Soldier
and the Stingy Woman

A SOLDIER CAME BACK ONE DAY FROM DRILLING WITH the troops in the field. He went to the hut where he had been ordered to spend the night.

In the cottage there lived an old woman.

"Good day in God's name, old woman," said the soldier. "Give me a little something to eat, will you?"

The old woman was angry at having another mouth to feed when there was scarcely food enough for herself. She answered, "See that little nail over there? Just hang yourself on it."

"I said I'm hungry, old woman. Give me some food! Are you deaf or something? Can't you hear?"

"Here, did you say?" said the old woman. "You might not like it much here. But you're welcome to find food and lodging somewhere else."

"You old witch," cried the soldier, "I'll cure your deafness for you!"

He was so hungry after a whole day of marching that he was even ready to go at her with his fists.

"Put something on the table!" he said.

"But there's nothing to eat in the house, dearie," said the stingy old woman. "Not a morsel to put in your mouth."

"Boil up a soup," said the soldier. "I'm very hungry."

"But from what, dearie?" asked the old woman.

"Just give me an axe," demanded the soldier, "and I'll boil up a soup out of that."

"Here's something to see!" thought the old woman. "I'll just keep my eyes open and see how a soldier makes soup out of an axe."

So she brought the soldier an axe. The soldier took it, put it in a pot, poured in water, and set it boiling. He let it boil and boil.

Then, after a while, he tasted it and said, "It's not quite right. Just put an onion in, will you?"

The old woman brought out an onion and put it in the pot.

The soldier boiled it some more. Then he tasted it and said, "Hmm, a bit too much on the onion side now. Bring some carrots and everything will be fine."

So the old woman added some carrots. The soup went on boiling.

In a while the soldier tasted it again. "It's soup now!" he exclaimed. "No one would take it for anything else. But a bit of meat would improve it."

The old woman rummaged around and brought out a piece of meat. She even found a bone. She added them to the pot. The soldier let the soup boil some more.

Then the old woman began to get impatient. She wanted to find out what axe soup was like.

"Let's taste it now," she said, bringing out the bowls. "It must be ready."

"Oh, it's ready all right," said the soldier. "But you'd better pour in some barley to finish it off properly."

The old woman poured the barley in.

Then the soldier stirred the pot a few more times and announced, "Well, old woman, it's all ready. Just bring out the bread and salt. Get hold of a spoon and we can eat the soup."

The old woman and the soldier began to eat up the soup. Soon they were nearly at the bottom of the pot. Then the old woman asked, "Soldier, when are we going to eat up the axe?" She wondered how a boiled axe would taste.

The soldier poked in the pot with his spoon.

"Hmm," he said. "The axe isn't really very tender yet. It needs more boiling. I'll just take it along when I leave in the morning. Then I can cook it some more tomorrow. Somewhere along the march I'll finish it up."

So the soldier put the axe in his sack, lay down in the corner, and went to sleep.

The next day he said good-bye to the old woman and moved on to the next village with the other troops.

And that's how the soldier tricked the stingy old woman. He got a good meal and carried off a new axe along with it!

Not Bad — But It Could Be Better

ONCE THERE WAS A WEALTHY LANDOWNER WHO LIVED in town. A peasants' village was part of the landowner's estate.

The peasants who worked for the landowner lived out in the country and took care of his property while he was off in the city.

One day the head man of the village, a peasant named Afonka, came to town to give a report to his master.

"Is that you, Afonka Petrov?" said the landowner, when he heard that a peasant had arrived from his village. "Come in."

"Good day, sir," said the peasant, taking off his cap.

"I hope you've brought good news from home, Afonka Petrov."

"Oh, yes, sir, yes indeed!"

"Well, speak up then! How are things in the village?"

"Not bad, sir. They're not bad at all."

"Anything special to report?"

"Well, no, sir, nothing very special," Afonka said. "Things are all right, you see."

"Well, good! Did you bring any letters from my mother?"

"Well, as to that, sir," said the peasant, twisting his cap in his hands, "I didn't."

"Didn't my mother write even a note for me? Maybe she isn't well?"

"Oh, no, sir! She could write well enough. It's only her leg that's a bit twisted, you see."

"Her leg's twisted! How did that happen?"

"Well, it just twisted, sir. It got turned, you know, the wrong way, and it twisted. That's all."

"Hmm, there must be more to it than that, Afonka. And why didn't Mother write to me about it?"

"Well, sir, things aren't bad, as I say, not bad . . . But they could be a bit better. There's no paper anymore, not a scrap. But we saved the pens, that we did."

"Saved the pens? Saved them from what?"

"Well, sir, as I said, things aren't bad, but they could be better. The paper was all burned up."

"All burned up! How did that happen?" the landowner asked. "Someone dropped a candle in the office, I suppose, and burned the papers?"

"Oh, no, sir! No one dropped a candle! That would be careless, it would indeed. No one burned the papers. It was the office that was burning. The papers just caught on fire by chance, being inside the office."

"What! The office was burning?"

"Well, you might say so, sir, it was. Things aren't bad, though, not bad at all. We saved the pens and a lantern before the office fell down."

"Fell down! Then you mean to say the office burned right to the ground! And you say no one was careless! Someone must have knocked over a candle in the office!"

"Oh, no, sir! There was no candle. The office caught fire from the storehouse. How could you think we were careless with the candles?"

"The storehouse! You mean the office caught on fire and—and the storehouse, too?"

"Oh, no, sir! The storehouse caught fire first. Then the office. The Lord must have been angry with us. But things aren't so bad."

"Not so bad! How can you say such a thing?" the landowner exclaimed.

"We saved something from the storehouse, sir."

"Well, that's a relief! What did you save?"

"Fourteen barrels of preserves and the sacks of grain," Afonka replied. "Of course, the building was done for."

"Done for?"

"Burned to the ground."

"Burned to the ground—along with the office! And I suppose you'll say that's not so bad!"

"Not bad at all, sir, when you come to think about it. Of course, it could be better. About those fourteen barrels of preserves—well, the tops were broken in. We ate what we could right away, but some of the preserves turned sour and you can't do much with them now. We pulled the grain out of the storehouse. But the sacks were all scorched. So I gave the grain to the peasants to make beer. It isn't bad, sir. It's very good beer."

"Who said you could give away my grain?" cried the wealthy landowner.

"And where could we have put the grain, sir, with the sacks all scorched and the storehouse burned to the ground?"

"You might have put the grain in the barn, you know."

"Well, sir, indeed, I would have been willing to do it, but there's no roof left on the barn."

"No roof left on the barn! What are you saying!"

"How could there be a roof, sir, when the barn walls caved in like that?"

"The walls caved in! You idiot! And you said there was nothing special to report! And that things weren't bad!" The landowner threw up his hands in despair. "All right, then—speak up! What happened to the barn?"

"Well, as I was saying, sir, nothing really happened to the barn. It was the storehouse that caught fire first, you see. Then the fire spread to the office. And I guess it spread to the barn, too, because the whole thing caught fire—it did indeed! That's why the walls caved in. So now there's no barn roof left either. The Lord must have been angry with us."

"So it wasn't just the papers in the office at all. The office is gone, and the storehouse is gone—and now you say the barn, too! And things aren't so bad in the village!" The landowner clutched his head.

"Well, they could be better, sir, they could indeed." The peasant twisted his cap around again. "But when you think about it, it's not really so bad."

"Not really so bad, eh!"

"No, sir, we saved some things."

"What did you save?"

"We pulled some of the timbers and posts out of the fire. Of course, they were all charred. So I gave the wood to the peasants."

"Of course! I suppose you didn't think of trying to save the animals. What about the work horses and the cows?"

"Oh, sir! We saved the animals—the horses, that is. We pulled them out of the barn."

"That's not so bad, then," the landowner said, relieved.

"Not so bad, sir, as I said, but it could be better. Someone tied the horses to a broken fence and they wandered away. We're not likely to get them back now. The cows are gone. But we saved the cat. We pulled the cat out and it didn't get away."

"The cat. What cat?"

"The house cat, sir, your mother's house cat."

"Very useful!"

"Indeed, sir, that cat is a very useful animal. It keeps the house free of mice, so they say. But I suppose there isn't much use for it now."

"Not much use for it? Why not?"

"Well, when you come to think of it, sir, most of the mice lived in the kitchen, but now with the kitchen gone—"

"The kitchen gone! And where did it go? You're not going to tell me the kitchen burned, are you?"

"Not the kitchen, sir, not all of it, at least not right away. It was the porch that caught on fire first."

"The porch of the manor house! On fire!"

"Yes, sir, after the barn, you know. But we saved some things. Some stair rails and a door."

"The stair rails!" roared the landowner, jumping up. "There is no stairway in the kitchen or on the porch! You must mean the whole manor house caught fire! You fool! And the kitchen! And the porch!"

"The porch first, sir, then the kitchen. After that the rest of the house started burning, too. It's only natural. The Lord must have been angry with us."

"You idiot!" shouted the landowner. "You must be drunk! How could you come in here and say there was nothing to report! And your eternal 'Things aren't so bad'! I'll teach you a thing or two about what's bad and what isn't!"

"Well, I admit it, sir," Afonka confessed, "things could be better. But we did our best and saved some things. As I was saying, there are those parts of the stairway. And the door. And we saved your mother, sir, we really did. And we have her cat, too, safe and sound from the barn. Of course, the cat's fur is a little burnt and its whiskers singed off. But it will catch mice again, once the house and the barn and the office and the storehouse are rebuilt."

"A fine lot of things you saved! Charred timbers! And my barrels of preserves spoiled or eaten!

The grain given away to make beer! The horses gone, and the cows finished! Well, at least you got my mother out unharmed."

"We did, sir, we certainly did. There's just one more thing to tell. The stairway was burning, so we had to throw your mother out the window."

"Out the window! But you should have called over the other peasants to catch her."

"I did, sir, but none of them would stand underneath the window to try it. Excuse me, sir, but your mother is well fed—bread and potatoes one hundred percent, as they say—and she'd be likely to crush anyone standing underneath. So we had to throw her out directly, just like that. And that's how she twisted her leg. Of course, it wouldn't have been so bad if it were just the leg, you know, no one minds that. But she had to go and fall on her head and—"

"*Stop!*" shouted the landowner as he sat back down again. "Go on back, Afonka, go back to the village. I can't stand any more of your good news!"

Hungry-for-Battle

A PEASANT WAS PLOWING A FIELD ONE DAY. HIS NAME was Hungry because he was so thin. The peasant's plow horse was skinny as a rail, and lame to boot. They didn't make a very impressive pair.

It was a hot day. As soon as Hungry and his horse started moving along the furrows, the horse was covered with flies and swarms of gnats. So the peasant took out his long whip and snapped it.

He tossed the whip around so quickly and aimed so well — you wouldn't believe how well he did it — that in one blow he killed thirty-three flies and a huge swarm of gnats.

Now the peasant was not smart, but he had a good imagination and was easily pleased. He began to think about what he had done.

"I'm not strong, but my arm is long," he thought. "I ought to ride into battle with the best and bravest fighters. Here I've killed thirty-three valiant men with one blow. And you couldn't even count the light troops I've knocked off."

In a few minutes Hungry's imagination was working full speed. He dreamed up enough ideas to make himself feel very important. He unharnessed his horse from the plow. Then he climbed up on the animal — he nearly fell off once or twice — and sat there as much like a real rider as he could.

"No more plowing fields for me!" thought Hungry.

Everything was all right as long as the horse was standing still. But then the horse started moving. Hungry turned his horse away from the field and jounced out on the highroad. He jolted to a stop, tumbled off, and cut down a sapling.

Then he set up a post with this sign on it: "Hungry-for-Battle, the great warrior, passed this way. On this spot Hungry met a force of pagan Tatars. He knocked off thirty-three warriors with one blow. (He couldn't even keep track of the light troops he did in.) If some warrior is going the opposite way, wait for Hungry here by the post. If someone comes riding the same way, catch up with the great warrior."

Hungry climbed up on his nag again and ambled off without hurrying, since he wasn't sure where he was really going.

A little later, someone came riding by the sign. He was a real fighter, a famous warrior named Churila. He read the sign and was surprised. He had never heard of Hungry-for-Battle.

But the man sounded fierce, so Churila didn't wait by the post but hurried on to catch up with

Hungry. It was clear enough that Hungry-for-Battle
was a great warrior. Thirty-three Tatars with one
blow! It would be good to make friends with a
fighter like that.

Churila urged his horse on, galloping as fast
as he could until he came up behind Hungry. What

was that? A fire poker riding a fence rail?

Churila came up alongside the skinny horse and rider and asked, "Have you seen a warrior come by this way? Someone named Hungry-for-Battle?"

"I have," said Hungry. "I myself am Hungry-for-Battle. Who are you?"

"I am Churila," answered the young warrior, "Churila Plenkovich." And he bowed in greeting.

But all the while Churila was thinking, "What kind of joke is this? He's just a skinny peasant. And look at that bag of bones he's trying to sit on. It's a disgrace even to ride next to him. Just look at him! He shakes in the saddle like a stalk of grain in the wind. And that nag can barely drag its feet along."

"Well," said Hungry, "let's get down to business. Ride over there on my left."

Churila, still wondering what to do, pulled up and rode alongside him.

"Hungry-for-Battle!" thought Churila. "He looks more as if he's hungry for bread and meat." And he kept looking over at him curiously, but without letting Hungry notice. He kept an eye on the horse, too, expecting it to fall right out from under its rider at every step.

Meanwhile another warrior named Eruslan came riding by the signpost. He stopped to read it.

Then he galloped on, hurrying his horse along to catch up with Hungry-for-Battle.

In a few minutes Eruslan caught up with the two riders. When he saw that one of the men was his friend Churila, he was pleased. Eruslan and Churila had shared many dangers and were about equally famous.

Eruslan greeted his old friend, "Hey there, Churila! Have you seen the warrior Hungry-for-Battle?"

Churila silently pointed to his companion.

Eruslan bowed. He bowed lower than usual to hide how surprised he was.

"Ride up into line," ordered Hungry. "On the right!"

Just then, one more warrior caught up with them. This warrior was named Bova, the Princess's son. He had read the sign, too, and had hurried to catch up with the famous warrior, the great conqueror of the Tatar horde.

And what did Bova see? A peasant dragging himself along the road on a tired old nag! Could this be Hungry-for-Battle? But beside him were two famous warriors, Eruslan Lazarevich and Churila Plenkovich. And both of them were talking respectfully to the poor peasant.

Bova even heard Hungry say to his two companions, "I'm pleased to have you come along, friends."

So Bova, the son of a princess, bowed to Hungry, too, and waited to introduce himself.

"I am Hungry-for-Battle," said the peasant, "and I know my own size. And who are you?"

"His own size!" thought Bova. "If that's what he knows, then he doesn't know much."

Then Bova introduced himself. "I am Bova, the son of a princess."

"You are welcome to share in my famous exploits," said Hungry. "It's not too late. It's not too early either. Ride over there by Eruslan!"

So the three famous warriors rode along with Hungry.

They hadn't gone much farther before they came to the forbidden meadow of the Maiden Tsar. This Maiden Tsar was a beautiful woman, but she was a mighty warrior, too. She rode without a saddle and was an expert fighter. She carried weapons and commanded soldiers, and she knew how to use them to defend her lands against strangers.

Eruslan recognized the boundaries of the Maiden Tsar's kingdom. "That way is forbidden," he said. "These lands belong to the Maiden Tsar."

Churila explained that any invaders in those lands were certain to be killed. The Maiden Tsar had absolute power over everyone in her kingdom. Her people fought for her to the death.

"That's no problem!" said Hungry. "The Russian ruler can keep a lot of people under her heel, but she can't tell *us* where to go. Just ride your horses out onto the meadow."

"Hungry-for-Battle!" Eruslan exclaimed. "Think it over! The queen has a large force and good fighters. Twenty-two armed knights, all with the best weapons. And that's not all she has. Have you ever heard of Zilant? Zilant is a flying serpent, the brother of Tugarin the dragon."

"Oh, well!" said Hungry. "That's too small for me to bother with. But maybe it's the right size for you. You just take over, Eruslan. I'd kill them all off like flies and spoil it for you."

"Well, all right, then, it's settled!" said Eruslan. "If you'll back us up, let's go ahead and enjoy the forbidden meadow. We'll meet the Maiden Tsar's knights, too, I'm sure of that."

So the companions rode into the fields. They galloped across the lovely meadow covered with thick green grass and red and yellow field flowers. In the middle of the meadow they found a white tent. No one was inside. The warriors let their horses graze and rest. Then the men went into the tent, sat down, and kept a lookout from there.

Hungry-for-Battle was the only one who really lay down to rest. So as not to be too hot, he took off his shirt and hung it over the tent pole at the entrance to keep the sun off. Soon he started snoring soundly.

"Hungry-for-Battle must be sure of himself!" said Bova, the Princess's son.

Meanwhile a great alarm was raised at the Maiden Tsar's palace. The soldiers rang the bells, tooted on the trumpets, and shouted. Everyone seized weapons and brought out the horses. The sound of clanking swords and spears and the neighing of the horses was enough to wake the dead.

But Hungry slept on peacefully.

Then the gates of the city opened and out rode a troop of mounted soldiers and three warrior-knights in armor.

Churila woke up Hungry. "Get up! There's a big force coming out against us," he cried.

Hungry got up, yawning since he was still half-asleep, and asked how many men there were. Then he said, "What does that amount to? Three knights are just three bothersome flies, and the troops on horses are no worse than a bunch of gnats. I killed thirty-three with one blow."

Then Hungry grumbled to himself, "They won't let me finish my nap. They go waking me up for a trifle like that! Are they afraid?"

Hungry gave out orders. "Move along there, Churila, and meet them. Don't leave anyone out."

Then he added, "Wait a minute! Just spare one soldier to send to the lady warrior. Have him give her this message: 'You ought to marry me!' It's me I mean, Hungry-for-Battle."

Churila rode out. He fought for a long time, striking and cutting until he had cut down all the enemy except for the one man he sent back to the Maiden Tsar.

But for an answer she sent back six knights with three regiments of soldiers on horseback.

So Hungry's companions woke him up again, for by that time he had fallen asleep once more.

"Ha!" exclaimed Hungry. "You call that a strong army? I could lay them all flat with one wave of my arm. You there, what's-your-name, the Princess's son! Go out and do the job alone. But remember to leave one man to send to the Maiden Tsar. I'm still trying to get my message through." After saying that, Hungry went back to sleep.

With a little luck and good planning Bova knew he could triumph. First he set himself against the knights. He made them chase him, stringing them out behind him by riding faster and faster. Then suddenly he turned and rode back along the line, cutting down the knights in a row, one after another.

This done, Bova turned his attention to the mounted soldiers. He spun his horse around and jumped into the middle of the troops. The mounted soldiers were so amazed by this daring maneuver that they ran off in all directions instead of standing and fighting together. So Bova circled his horse around the confused men and defeated them one by one. Then the victorious Bova went back to Hungry's tent to rest.

But the Maiden Tsar sent out an even bigger force after that. This time there were twelve warriors and six regiments of mounted troops. The knights galloped across the meadow toward the white tent, shouting, trumpeting, and waving their swords.

"Oh, ho!" said Hungry, getting up again. "Look at that! It's grains of dust blowing across the field!" Then he looked again. "Watch out! That's not dust — it's twelve pesky flies and no end of gnats."

Then he called the third companion over. "Eruslan! Will you take over? If you have any trouble we'll lend a hand."

Eruslan mounted his horse, reared up, and shot off like a hawk. His method was surprise. The knights expected him to work according to some strategy, but he flew straight into the middle of the company with his sturdy sword stretched out in front of him, chopping and hacking in all directions. First to the left, then to the right; next he would turn to finish off someone attacking from behind or bend down to get someone from below. The mounted troops scattered and fell under the weight of his sword.

When even the strongest force of knights and soldiers didn't come back alive, the Maiden Tsar saw she was in trouble. She couldn't hold back anything if she wanted to avoid a disaster. It was time to send out Zilant, the flying serpent.

Zilant's scales were like so many shields hung together on a huge moving wall. He roared and rumbled like a thunderstorm as he rose up out of his iron nest. The nest alone was so big it was hung from twelve tall oaks by twelve great chains.

Zilant flew through the sky like an arrow shot from a huge bow. He called out as he flew, demanding a challenger to come out and meet him in a fight to the death.

"Hmm," thought Hungry, "it looks as if it's my turn. I'm all out of helpers. Well, I can't do a thing about it, I guess. I'm riding straight to the grave, that's what I'm doing." For Hungry was not so stupid as to believe he could handle the flying serpent. He felt a little sad about the whole thing.

And he felt sorry for himself and sorry for letting down his friends.

"It's the end of my hide, a blow for my side, and a shame to my pride," he thought. "Hmm, not a bad rhyme for a man about to die."

Hungry made the sign of the cross, mounted his nag, and slowly ambled off away from the tent. He had his eyes squeezed shut because he couldn't stand to see what was coming, but he waved his axe in the air as much as he could.

Zilant saw Hungry from far off and gave a loud roar. Then he roared again and flew in closer. But he stopped short, right under a cloud, when he saw Hungry up close.

"They've sent him out as a joke!" the flying serpent thought.

Meanwhile Hungry was whispering to himself, "Fathers, brothers, and the holy saints — don't forget my name up there!"

Expecting death any minute, Hungry let his head fall to the neck of his little horse. The horse was running along on three legs and dragging the other along. He was always lame anyway, and now he was tired, too.

Zilant's eyes nearly popped out of his head. "There must be a plot behind it," he thought. "The little peasant is lying down on his horse.

He's going to sleep! What kind of warrior is that? If I snapped my fingers he'd fly five yards away."

Zilant flew down to look closer to see if there weren't some clever trap in it. He had to lean right down to the saddle to get a good look.

Just then, feeling the serpent's breath on his neck, Hungry raised his head. Suddenly he was filled with courage. He gave out such a whack with his axe that Zilant crashed to the ground.

Right on the spot, without giving the dazed serpent time to come to its senses, Hungry started to chop it up the way he used to chop pine trees into sticks of kindling. When there was nothing left of the serpent but little pieces, he waved his axe in the air, sliced back and forth with it, took off his hat, and rode back to his friends.

"Hail to the great champion!" the three warriors shouted from the tent.

After that, the Maiden Tsar had to order the city gates opened. She invited the warriors into the palace.

"A tasty feast, and they'll make peace," she thought. But when she saw Hungry she couldn't get over it. "The strangest things are strong as iron," the Maiden Tsar said to herself.

She went up to Hungry and greeted him the way rulers are greeted, by putting her hand on his shoulder. It was a heavy hand because she was a warrior.

The weight of her hand pressed Hungry down so that he could hardly move a muscle. But he made an effort, broke away, shook himself, and bowed to the Maiden Tsar.

She spoke, "I bid the glorious hero welcome. I have always had respect for courage."

She shook Hungry's hand. All Hungry's bones rattled like stones in an empty kettle, but he clenched his teeth together to keep from moaning.

"Defend my realm!" the Maiden Tsar shouted in his ear. "You alone must guard us."

Hungry bowed again. He was much more worried about how to defend his head from the Maiden Tsar at that point.

The mighty woman then ordered the servants to bring out strong mead for their talks. She thought she would give her guests a trial and see if they were strong at the table as well as on the battlefield.

But Hungry was in no mood for a feast. He had no appetite, and he didn't touch the food or drink the mead.

"When I've finished my work, I don't drink anything but a warrior's magic water," he announced.

Hungry knew that warrior's water gave great

strength to those who drank it. The Maiden Tsar must have some. Otherwise how did she get to be so strong?

"We have warrior's water," said the Maiden Tsar.

"But do you have a lot?" asked Hungry.

"A full bottle," she answered.

"But is it really good, your water?" asked Hungry. "Most bottles aren't worth drinking a glassful."

"Try it out!" said the Maiden Tsar. And she ordered her servants to bring in a full bottle of warrior's water and a golden cup to go with it.

Hungry poured out a cupful, drank it, and felt good. Now he really had some strength to go with his long arm!

The Maiden Tsar wanted to know how he liked the water.

"I haven't quite caught the taste yet," said Hungry, and he poured out another cup. He drank three more cupfuls, one after another.

"That's enough, that's enough!" shouted the lady warrior. "You aren't leaving any for me!"

"Wonderful water!" said Hungry, strutting around and flinging his arms out in all directions. "Let's see how strong I am now!"

Hungry had the Maiden Tsar's servants bring

in a heavy ship's rope. He made a loop in it, tied a strong knot, and hung it up. Then he had them bring a real war-horse out from the Maiden Tsar's stables. He mounted it, rode around turning and prancing, and then galloped up fast to the noose. He dropped his head into the loop while the horse was running at full speed.

He half expected his body to ride on ahead without his neck and head, but the magic water worked! The heavy rope broke.

Then Hungry took down the rope, made another loop, and lassoed the cupola on the palace church. Everyone was astounded at such strength.

But Churila, Eruslan, and Bova all shrugged their shoulders. "You should have seen him out there with Zilant!" they said. "He fooled the serpent and then ground him down into dust."

From then on, Hungry was a real honest-to-goodness warrior. He still looked as if he needed bread and meat, but he got himself fine weapons and rich clothes and married the Maiden Tsar.

She bore him two daughters, Smeta and Udacha, which mean "Skill" and "Success." Whenever Hungry looked at them he was very proud. They represented the best kind of skill and success a man could have. And no one ever even suspected that he had never killed thirty-three warriors with one blow.

The Peasant, the Bear, and the Fox

ONCE THERE LIVED A PEASANT AND A BEAR WHO WERE great friends. Indeed, one day they even decided to sow turnips together.

The peasant and the bear went out into the fields and sowed the turnips. Then they had to decide who should take what.

The peasant said, "I'll take the roots."

"But what do I get?" asked the bear.

"You get the tops, Misha," the peasant answered.

The turnips came up. The peasant took the roots for himself, and Misha the bear got the tops, as they had agreed.

Misha saw he had made a mistake. He growled and said to the peasant, "All right, my friend! You tricked me. Next time we sow something, you won't fool me like that!"

A year passed, and it was planting time again. The peasant said to the bear, "Come on, Misha, let's sow some wheat."

"All right," said the bear. But he was determined not to be cheated again.

Before long the wheat ripened. The stalks were golden yellow. The peasant said to the bear, "Now, Misha! Which part do you want? The root or the top?"

"Oh, no! my friend," said the bear, "you won't fool me this time! Just give me the root, and take the top for yourself." So when they gathered in the wheat, that's how it was divided.

The peasant took home the grains, ground them into flour, and baked a whole basketful of white rolls. Then, when he went back into the forest to cut wood, he brought the rolls to Misha the bear and said, "Look here, Misha! You see how well these nice tops turned out?"

"All right, friend peasant!" growled the bear. "You tricked me again! These roots are no good. Now I am very angry and I'll just eat *you*!"

The bear began to sharpen his claws on a tree. Seizing his chance the peasant jumped into his wood cart and hid as best he could behind the logs. Then the peasant started to cry.

A fox trotted up, saw the peasant, and asked,

"Why are you hiding and why are you crying?"

"Why shouldn't I cry—I'm frightened!" said the peasant. "The bear wants to eat me up!"

"Don't be afraid, uncle," said the fox. "He won't eat you. I have a plan."

The fox ordered the peasant to stay right in the same place. Then he went off into the bushes and imitated a hunter's voice.

He called to the peasant from the bushes: "Hey there! Woodsman! Are there any wild animals near here? Fierce-faced wolves or mean-mugged bears? I've got my gun ready!"

When the bear heard that he thought the hunters had really come. He crept up to the peasant and said, "Don't say a word about me—I won't eat you."

The peasant replied to the fox, "Not a single animal here."

The bear kept close to the peasant's cart. He did not want to risk meeting a hunter.

The fox called again: "No animals! Then what's that lying by your wagon over there?"

The bear whispered to the peasant, so as not to attract attention, "Say that it's a big chunk of wood."

"It's a big chunk of wood!" called the peasant.

"If it were a chunk of wood," said the fox, "it would be tied up with rope along with the other logs."

Then the fox ducked down low among the bushes and moved to another place.

The bear said to the peasant, "Tie me up along with the other logs! And hurry!"

The peasant did just that.

Then the fox popped up in another place. Using a different voice he cried, "Hey, woodsman! We're looking for game. Are there any wild animals here, fierce-faced wolves or mean-mugged bears? We've all got guns!"

"Not a one!" said the peasant.

"But what is that lying by your wagon over there?"

"A chunk of wood."

"Are you sure it isn't a bear? If it were a chunk

of wood you would be hitting it with your axe!"

The bear whispered to the peasant, "Hit me with your axe!"

The peasant did just that. He whacked the bear with the flat of his axe, and the bear was knocked senseless. Now the peasant could get in his wagon and safely go home.

Was the peasant grateful to the fox for having helped him out? Just wait!

The fox went over to the peasant.

"Now, friend peasant," he said, "what will you give me for my work?"

"I'll give you a pair of white hens," said the peasant. Then he went behind his cart and returned with a sack.

"Carry them away," the peasant told the fox. "But don't peek."

The fox took the sack from the peasant and went away. He carried the sack on and on. Then he thought, "Oh, come now! I'll have just a little peek."

The fox peeked — and there, inside the sack, were two white dogs, not hens!

The dogs jumped right out of the sack and started chasing the fox. The fox ran and ran.

He ran under a stump and down into a hole, where he was safe. He felt very clever indeed for having outwitted the dogs.

The dogs waited at the entrance to the hole. But the fox just laughed at them.

Soon the fox found himself arguing with the dogs.

"You're good for nothing!" said the dogs. "You can't do anything right."

"Yes, I can!" answered the fox. "I got away from you. And I can do all kinds of things."

"What can your ears do?" asked the dogs.

"Listen!" answered the fox. "My ears listen."

"And your feet, what can they do?"

"Run!" answered the fox. "My feet can run fast."

"How about your eyes?"

"My eyes!" said the fox. "They keep a lookout."

"What about your tail?" asked the dogs.

"My tail!" said the fox. "Hmm, when I'm running as fast as I can, my tail gets in the way, I have to admit that."

"You see!" said the dogs.

"But I can fix that!" said the fox. "Just watch how I get rid of it!"

And the fox threw his tail out of the hole.

The dogs caught hold of it, dragged out the fox along with it, and ate him up.

Yes, animals are sometimes stupid. But men are ungrateful.

The Cat and the She-Fox

ONCE UPON A TIME THERE LIVED A PEASANT WHO
had a cat. But — what a shame! — it was such a
mischievous cat that the peasant had had enough
of him.

The peasant thought it over. How was he to
get rid of the animal? Finally he took the cat, sat
him in a sack, and tied the sack up. He carried the
sack a long way and then threw it deep into the
dark forest.

"Let him get lost!" the peasant thought.

The cat wasn't very big. He just slid right out
of the sack and looked around. Then he started
walking. He walked and walked until finally he
found a little hut where a forester lived. So he
climbed up into the little attic of the hut and made
a home for himself there.

The cat spent whole days doing what he pleased.
When he was hungry he would go through the for-

est to hunt birds and mice. He would fill himself up until his little belly was like a round ball. Then he would go back to the attic. He didn't have a thing to worry about!

One day the cat was out taking a walk when a she-fox came along the other way. She took one look at the cat and from surprise stopped in her tracks.

"What a strange little animal!" she thought. "I've lived in the forest for years, but I've never seen a beast like that!"

She bowed to the cat politely and asked, "How do you do, sir, and who are you? How did you get here? By what name shall we call you?"

The cat puffed up his fur, stretched himself out as big as he could, and answered, "I am sent here from the Siberian forests to be the boss. I am in charge of things now. My name is Katafat Ivanovich. But you may call me Kat."

"Oh, my! Katafat Ivanovich!" said the fox. "I'm sorry to have to ask such silly questions, but I wasn't expecting you. No one told me you were coming here. But I hope you won't think we aren't friendly. Let me invite you to be a guest at my house."

So the cat turned around and followed the she-fox. She led him to her burrow and made a regular feast of different game birds for him. And she got some information from him, too.

"Excuse me, Kat," she said, "but are you married or a bachelor?"

The cat finished a piece of quail and took a bite of wood duck.

"A bachelor," he said.

"Well," said the she-fox, "I am a she-fox, a free fox, so marry me."

The cat agreed. And all that evening there was feasting and fun in the burrow.

The next day the fox went out to get supplies so there would be something for her new husband to eat. The cat stayed home.

The fox was running along when suddenly she met the wolf going the other way. The wolf began to tease her. He had a way of picking on the smaller animals. "Wherever have you been, little gossip?" the wolf asked. "We searched around all the burrows but we didn't see you. You know we can't have fun without you."

"Let me be, you blockhead!" the fox replied. "Why are you always teasing? When I played games with you I was a she-fox, a free fox, but now I'm a true wife, wedded for life."

The wolf was surprised. "Whom did you marry, Lizaveta Ivanovna?"

"You mean you haven't heard about Katafat?

Katafat Ivanovich, who was sent to us from the Siberian forests to be in charge? Well, you'd better watch out, because I am the boss's wife now."

The wolf was suspicious. "No, I didn't hear about that, Lizaveta. No one ever said I wasn't in charge here. Just let me see what he looks like."

"See what he looks like!" exclaimed the fox. "Oooo! The new boss has such a temper — if someone doesn't suit him, he'll just eat him up!"

The wolf began to get worried.

"But watch your step and do as I tell you," said the fox, "and maybe you'll get by with only a scratch or two. First prepare a sheep and bring it back here to pay your respects to him. Put the sheep down near this tree, and lie low so he doesn't see you. Otherwise, wolf, you'll be in trouble!"

The wolf ran off to get the sheep.

The fox walked on alone. Then a bear met her going the other way.

"Why don't you come and play, Liza?" he said, cuffing her on the neck.

"Why are you pushing and shoving, you blockhead, you clumsy Mishka?" cried the fox. "When I played with you I was a she-fox, a free fox, but now I'm a true wife, wedded for life."

"What?" said the bear. "Whom did you marry, Liza?"

"I married the boss sent from the Siberian forests to take charge of things here. His name is Kata-fat Ivanovich, but now that we are married I call him Kat. That's who I married."

"The boss? Is that so!" said the bear. "Just let me get a look at him."

"A look at him!" squealed Liza. "You'd better

look after you own skin! Kat has such a temper, if
someone doesn't suit him or rubs him the wrong
way, he'll just eat him up on the spot!"

"He will?" said the bear slowly.

"Yes," said the fox. "If you want to see him,
Mishka, get going and prepare a bull. Then bring
it back here to pay your respects to him. The wolf
has decided to bring a sheep. And look sharp, you!
Don't just come crashing in. Put down the bull
near this tree and lie low so Kat won't see you.
Otherwise, my boy, you'll be in trouble!"

The bear lumbered off to get the bull, trying
to remember everything Liza had told him.

The wolf brought the sheep to the appointed
place, took off the skin, and stood there thinking
hard. After a while he looked up and saw the bear
coming along with a bull.

"Hello, brother bear, Mikhailo," said the wolf.

"Hello, brother Levon!" said the brown bear.
"Haven't you seen the she-fox and her husband?"

"No, brother," answered the wolf. "And I've
been waiting a long time."

"You run along and call them," said the bear.

"Oh, no! I won't go, Mikhailo! You go. You're
much braver than I am."

"No, brother Levon, I won't go either," said the
bear.

Just then a rabbit popped out and ran across the path. The bear called out to him, "Just come here, you cross-eyed rascal!"

The rabbit was frightened and came running up.

"Now then, you cross-eyed scamp, you know where the she-fox lives?"

"I do, Mikhailo!"

"Then be off in a hurry and tell her that Mikhailo the bear and his friend Levon the wolf were ready long ago. Tell her, 'They're waiting for you and your husband, wanting to pay their respects with a sheep and a bull.' "

The rabbit set off for the fox's burrow as fast as he could scamper. In the meantime, the bear and the wolf began to think up places where they might hide.

The bear said, "I'll climb up in the pine tree."

"And what am I to do?" asked the wolf. "Why, I can't climb a tree for anything! Mikhailo, brother Mishka, bury me under something or other — help me out!"

The bear hid the wolf in the bushes and piled dry leaves on him until he was covered. Then the bear climbed into the pine tree, to the very top. There he sat and took a look — when was Katafat going to come with the she-fox?

The rabbit, meanwhile, ran up to the she-fox's burrow, knocked twice, and said to Lizaveta, "Mikhailo and his friend Levon sent me to say that they were ready long ago, waiting for you and your husband. They want to pay you their respects with a bull and a sheep."

"Go along, then, cross-eyes! We'll be there right away!" called the fox.

And sure enough, along came the cat and the fox. From his hiding place the bear caught sight of them and called down to the wolf, "Hey, brother Levon, the fox is coming with her husband. How small he is! He isn't nearly as big as I thought he would be."

When the cat got to the tree he rushed straight for the bull. He hissed and growled, and his fur stood on end. He began to tear off hunks of meat with his teeth and claws. All the while he growled as if he were angry. "Not enough, not enough!" he hissed.

The bear saw and heard everything. He whispered down to the wolf, "He's not big but he has a huge appetite! Four of us couldn't eat that much, but for one of him it's not enough. He'll eat his way through to us, that's what he'll do!"

The wolf wished he could look at Katafat, but he couldn't see much from the bushes where he was hiding. So he began to dig away the leaves covering his eyes. The leaves rustled. The cat heard the rustling and thought it was a mouse. He jumped headlong, straight onto the wolf! He landed on the wolf's head, claws first.

The wolf jumped up, howling, and ran for his life — and that was the last seen of him!

But Katafat was frightened, too, and he flew right into the tree where the bear was sitting.

"There!" thought the bear. "He's seen me!"

There was no time to climb down, so, counting on aid from heaven, he just let go and fell — smack! — on the ground.

The bear made a loud crash and bruised himself inside and out. He, too, jumped up and·ran.

The fox called out after them, "Wait up, there, you two! He'll really give it to you! Wait a minute!" But it was too late.

From that day on, all the animals were afraid of the cat. They reasoned none of them was bigger than the wolf and bear, and the wolf and bear had just barely escaped with their lives! The cat was the new boss of the forest, all right. He and the she-fox got in a store of meat for the whole winter and passed the time doing whatever they pleased.

And to this day the cat mews while he bites and chews.

Part Two:
Of Heroes and Heroines

The Firebird

IN THE THREE AND SEVENTH, THREE ELEVENTH KING-
dom there was a Tsar. The Tsar had three sons:
Peter Tsarevich, which means Peter the Tsar's son,
Dmitry Tsarevich, and Ivan Tsarevich.

In the Tsar's garden grew an apple tree, and on
the tree grew golden apples. But one day the Tsar
noticed that every night one of the apples disap-
peared. After a while there weren't many apples left.

So the Tsar called his sons together. He said,
"My dear children! If you love me, keep a lookout
for the thief. If one of you catches him, I will give
him half a kingdom."

The first night the oldest brother, Peter, went
out to the garden. He kept watch until twelve
o'clock, but after midnight he fell asleep. When he
woke the next morning and looked at the tree, one
apple was gone! He went in to his father and told
him everything that had happened.

The next night the middle brother, Dmitry, went to the garden to keep watch. But he too fell asleep after midnight, and he woke the next morning to find an apple missing from the tree.

The third night the youngest brother, Ivan, began begging for permission to go out and keep watch in the garden. But his father wouldn't agree to it.

"You're too young," the Tsar said. "Something might happen to you and you'll be frightened."

But the youngest son asked so much that his father finally agreed to let him go.

So Ivan went into the garden and sat down under the apple tree. It seemed he hadn't been sitting there very long when suddenly the whole garden was filled with light.

Ivan Tsarevich looked up, and there it was! A firebird was streaking down into the garden. The bird's plumage was all gold, and silver sparks flashed from her claws. Her crested head and the long tail feathers were gold mixed with curving plumes of brilliant red and orange. As the bird flew, the feathers and plumes flashed and glowed. The firebird made such a bright light in the sky — more like a burning meteor or a falling star than a bird — that any watcher could hardly keep his eyes on it.

Ivan Tsarevich had never seen such a beau-

tiful sight in all his father's kingdom. He ran and hid under the golden apple tree.

The firebird flew into the garden and landed on a branch. The bird's light covered the tree like a shower of sparks, and the apples shone more brightly than ever before.

The firebird was just about to pull an apple from the tree when Ivan crept up to her. He moved carefully, reached out, and grabbed her by the tail.

"Caught!" he exclaimed happily.

But the bird tore herself away and flew off.

All the same, Ivan had one feather left in his hand. He wrapped the feather in a scarf and stayed in the garden until dawn. The golden rays of the sun at dawn were no brighter than the firebird's wings.

Ivan went to his father.

The Tsar asked, "Well, my dearest son, did you see the thief?"

"I did," Ivan answered, and unrolled the scarf. The feather glowed and gave light to the whole room.

"Ah!" said the Tsar. "Ivan! What kind of bird has feathers like that? I've never seen anything like it in all my kingdom."

Then the Tsar called his other two sons. "My dear children," he said, "the thief has been seen but not caught. I want you to do something for me right away. I want you to go on a journey and find this firebird. To the one who finds her I'll give a whole kingdom."

The two eldest brothers got ready to leave, but the Tsar wouldn't let his youngest son go. Ivan asked and begged harder than before. The Tsar refused to agree for a long time, but at last he gave in and blessed all three sons. The three young men rode away together.

They rode on and on — it was hard to say whether the time was long or short — until they came to a signpost. Three roads led from the signpost in different directions.

The signpost had three messages on it. That pointing to the righthand road said, "Death is at the end." That to the left, "Hunger is waiting for you." The middle way read, "Starvation is watching for you and your horse."

The brothers stopped and thought. Who should go which way? All three roads were forbidding.

At length the brave youngest brother chose the righthand road. Peter and Dmitry said they would go along the two remaining roads.

Ivan Tsarevich rode on for a long time. Finally he came to a little hut. It was a very unusual place. The hut stood on chicken legs, and it kept hopping back and forth and turning around and about.

A strange sight indeed! Behind it stood a tall oak.

But Ivan Tsarevich knew what to do. He went up to the hut and said,

"Little hut! Little hut! One, two, three!

Turn your front door to me

And your back to the tree!"

Sure enough, the little hut turned its front door toward Ivan Tsarevich.

Ivan went inside the hut. Upon the stove lay Baba Yaga, the bone-legged witch. Baba Yaga and her family were the wickedest witches in the whole Russian forest.

Baba Yaga pushed her nose up against the roof of the hut and screamed from up on the stove at the top of her voice, "What's gotten in here? Something smells like a Russian!"

Ivan called back to her, "Just watch out, you old devil! I'll pull you down from the stove. You can't scare me. I'll give it to you with a stick on all your bones!"

Baba Yaga jumped down from the stove and started pleading for mercy. "Good young lad," she said, "don't beat me. I'll do some favor for you."

Ivan said, "Why start shouting at me? You'd better give me some food and something to drink and then find me a place to sleep. What bad manners you have!"

Then Baba Yaga asked, "Who are you?"

The young man answered, "I am Ivan Tsarevich."

Baba Yaga gave him something to eat and drink right away. Then she gave him a place to sleep.

The next morning Ivan Tsarevich woke up, washed, dressed, said his prayers, and started asking some questions.

"Do you know where I can find the firebird, Baba Yaga?"

"I don't know myself," she answered, "but you just ride on farther and you'll find my middle sister. She'll tell you. And here's an old boot heel for you. When you are bringing back the firebird they'll chase after you. Then you say, 'Little heel, little heel! Change into a mountain!' It will change into a mountain and you can go on."

Ivan thanked her heartily and set off to find her sister.

He rode on for a while when suddenly, there by the road, he spied another little hut on chicken legs, turning and hopping around.

Ivan Tsarevich said,

"Little hut! Little hut! One, two, three!
Turn your front door to me
And your back to the tree!"

The hut turned its front door to him and Ivan

entered. On the stove lay Baba Yaga, the middle-aged, bone-legged witch. Her nose was jammed into the roof. She shouted, "What's gotten in here that smells like a Russian?"

"Watch out!" said Ivan. "I'll pull you down from the stove and beat every bone you've got."

But the middle witch jumped down from the stove, gave Ivan something to eat and drink, and found him a bed.

In the morning Ivan got up and asked, "Where is the firebird?"

"Ride on farther to my eldest sister," she told him. Then she gave him a comb. "When you get the firebird," she said, "they'll chase you. But take out the comb and say, 'Little comb, little comb! Turn into a dense forest!' The comb will do this and you can ride away."

Ivan thanked her heartily and set off to find the eldest sister. He rode on a while and soon, there by the road, was still another hut on chicken legs.

"Little hut! Little hut! One, two, three!
Turn this way!"
said Ivan.

He went into the hut, and there lay the third Baba Yaga on the stove with her nose against the ceiling. She shouted, "What smells of Russian in here?"

But she got down from the warm stove, gave Ivan something to eat and drink, and found him a place to sleep.

In the morning Ivan got up, said his prayers, and asked about the firebird.

First Baba Yaga gave him a brush, saying, "When they chase you, say to the brush, 'Little brush, little brush! Turn into a fiery river!' The brush will do this and you can get away."

Ivan took the brush.

"Now listen," the witch continued. "When you get to the kingdom where the firebird lives, there will be a wall all around. In the wall will be gates, and behind the wall three cages will be hanging. In the golden cage sits a crow, in the silver cage a daw, and in the copper cage — the firebird. But remember! Don't take the silver cage or the gold one. And don't take the copper cage either. Open the little door, take out the firebird, and tie it up in a scarf."

Ivan Tsarevich thanked her for her advice and started out.

When he reached the kingdom of the firebird he rode right up and looked at the stone wall. There was no way of squeezing through. You couldn't get in by the gates either, because at the gates stood lions with their mouths wide open.

Ivan took one look at things and spoke to his

horse, "Listen, faithful horse! Do you see that wall? Come on now," he said, "jump over it and let me get the firebird."

The horse backed up to get a running start. He plunged forward and hup! went right over the wall.

But then there was more trouble. Ivan saw that the firebird was big and his scarf was small. He couldn't possibly wrap her up in it. So he thought it over and decided to take the whole copper cage.

But suddenly — the instant he touched the cage — bells started ringing everywhere, and the lions began roaring. It was a warning to the whole kingdom.

Ivan Tsarevich was afraid he might be caught. So, with the cage in his hand, he jumped on his horse, saying, "Let's go!"

The horse took another running start, leaped back over the wall, and galloped away as fast as he could.

Ivan hadn't gone far before he saw that riders were chasing after him, hot on his trail. He took out the boot heel. "Little heel, little heel! Turn into a mountain!" he said.

In an instant the heel turned into a mountain, just the way Baba Yaga said it would, and Ivan Tsarevich went riding off again.

The troops following him galloped up to the mountain, took one look, and saw how big the mountain was. They knew they could never ride across it, so they turned back and went home to get a load of shovels. They rode back to the mountain, shoveled it down flat, and started chasing after Ivan again.

When the young man saw that the horsemen were still after him, he took out the comb and said, "Little comb, little comb! Turn into a dense forest!" And it did.

The troops galloped up to the forest. They saw they couldn't ride through it, it was so thick. So they returned home, gathered together a pile of axes, rode back to the forest, and cut a road through the trees. Once more they galloped after Ivan.

When Ivan noticed he was still being followed, he took out the brush and spoke to it, "Little brush, little brush! Turn into a fiery river!"

Ivan certainly hoped the brush would work as the comb and heel had. His horse was tired and needed a rest.

As the troops closed the distance between themselves and Ivan, a fiery river spread out in front of them. Ivan Tsarevich was on the other bank, lying down with his hands behind his head. And he still had the firebird, safe in its copper cage.

The troops were furious. A few of them tried to back up and leap over the river. But the same thing always happened. The rider fell into the burning waters, and that was the end of him. The men thought of building a bridge over the flaming river, but they knew it would burn. The horsemen realized they couldn't do anything to prevent Ivan's escape, so they turned back.

Ivan Tsarevich rested a while longer and then rode away again.

But his troubles were not over yet. After a long ride he came back to that same signpost where the three roads met. A tent had been set up by the post, and two young men were sitting inside. When Ivan got closer he recognized them as his brothers, Peter and Dmitry. He was happy to see them, greeted them with affection, showed them the caged firebird, and told them everything that had happened. Then Ivan lay down in the tent to rest.

But the brothers were jealous that Ivan, the youngest son, would be bringing the firebird back to their father. "Ivan will be given a whole kingdom, and we older ones won't have anything," they said.

So Peter and Dmitry agreed to throw Ivan into a deep pit. While he was still drowsy they tossed him in.

The pit was an awful place. There were all kinds of insects and crawling things in it, and down in the hole Ivan couldn't even see the sunlight. And his brothers left him nothing to eat or drink.

But Ivan ate some earth to sustain himself and decided to dig his way out to the top. He started crawling up the sides of the pit, digging handholds on the way and inching higher and higher. Finally, as he made his way up the dirt walls, he caught a glimpse of sunlight.

Ivan kept pulling himself up and at last climbed out. He saw that his brothers had vanished, taking the firebird with them. Ivan rested near the pit and went on his way again.

The first place he came to was a city. Inside the city walls a crowd of people had gathered near a small lake. He went up to them and asked, "What is this? Why are you standing around the lake?"

"We're waiting for the six-headed serpent to crawl out," someone answered. "We're supposed to throw a maiden to him. But since he's already eaten all the girls in town, we have to throw the ruler's own daughter to him."

"I'm sorry to hear that!" said Ivan. "Could you show me where the ruler and his daughter are?"

Just then the ruler and his daughter came up to the lake. Ivan ran to him and cried, "Wait! I can save your daughter!"

The ruler said sadly, "There's no point in thinking about it with a serpent like this one. Six heads! You have never seen anything like it!"

But Ivan Tsarevich insisted, "I can save your daughter. Just have the people tie up three bunches of sticks."

They barely had time to tie up the sticks and bring them to Ivan when the serpent swam up. He whistled in various voices, gave a great roar, and was just about to open a few of his mouths when Ivan rushed forward. He struck off two heads with one bunch of sticks, two more with another bunch, and the last two heads with a third. So all six heads were chopped off.

The ruler was overcome with joy, and all the people cheered. The ruler rushed over to congratulate Ivan. He invited him to the palace. The city people were so happy that Ivan had conquered the monster that they started a feast then and there.

Well, the ruler's daughter was the kind of beauty you don't see very often in this world. So when the ruler made a marriage proposal, Ivan accepted. There was a wonderful wedding, and the people enjoyed another feast.

Then the ruler thought of asking Ivan Tsarevich where he was from. Ivan willingly answered, "I am the Tsar's own son."

So the ruler said, "Wouldn't you like to see your father? If you would, I'll give you two ravens. You can climb on them and ride home. When you get on, just tell the ravens, 'I am going to my own king-dom.' They'll take you right there with no detours."

Ivan accepted the offer and the ruler gave the ravens to the bride and groom. The two climbed on and flew away.

Meanwhile, Ivan's two older brothers had taken the firebird to their father. The Tsar was very happy to have the fabulous creature. But on the second day, the firebird turned into a crow. Peter and Dmitry were surprised, and their father was dis-mayed.

"What does it mean?" the Tsar asked. But he took the cage and hung it in his room anyway. So the bird hung there, just an ordinary crow.

But as Ivan started the flight back to his father, the crow suddenly became the firebird again. Now the Tsar was even more amazed.

Suddenly the father heard a noise. He looked out the window and saw two ravens flying toward him, carrying a man and a girl. The Tsar was frightened. He thought they must be coming after the firebird and that the creature had changed back to her real form because she knew her own people were on the way.

But as soon as the ravens flew in the window, Ivan Tsarevich and his bride leaped off. Ivan rushed to hug his father and ask forgiveness for having married without his permission.

Ivan's father could hardly recognize him. "Oh, my dear son!" the Tsar cried. "Why did you stay away for so long? Your brothers are already here. They found the firebird and brought her to me."

"No," Ivan said, "it wasn't my brothers who found her. I got the firebird myself. I started to bring the firebird back to our palace when I met Peter and Dmitry. My brothers wanted the bird for themselves, so they threw me into a pit when I was half asleep and took the firebird away."

Then Ivan told his father everything, exactly as it had happened. When the Tsar heard Ivan's story, he sent the two older sons out to take care of the cattle and he gave his kingdom to Ivan. Then he ordered a celebration the likes of which has never been seen!

Far into the night the people rejoiced. The firebird lighted up the palace courtyard and the happy faces of the Tsar, Ivan Tsarevich and his bride, and all the feasting guests.

Daughter and Stepdaughter

A MAN WHOSE WIFE HAD DIED AND LEFT HIM WITH A daughter, married a widow who also had a daughter. The first daughter was Luba, the second Nastya. So the family had two daughters who were about the same age even though they were not twins.

But the father and his new wife were not a bit alike. The father was loving but timid. The widow was hateful and bossy. She turned out to be a bad stepmother for Luba.

The father tilled the land near the edge of a great forest. While he was working in the fields, the stepmother and the two daughters would stay home and spin flax.

Luba was good-tempered and generous, but the stepmother grew to hate the sight of her sitting by the stove spinning and humming. Her own daughter was quarrelsome and spiteful, but the mother thought the world of her.

The stepmother began to complain that Luba did not work hard enough.

"Luba sits by the stove singing and her fingers lie idle," growled the stepmother. "The spindle and the wheel should be humming, not the girl."

Now this was not true. Luba loved to help her family, and she knew that work goes faster and better when you make it into fun.

But the stepmother kept on nagging. "If she sat alone, she would spin better," she said. "Husband, take her into the woods, to the forest hut! She'll do more spinning there."

Deep in the forest there was indeed a little hut made of clods of earth. Wood gatherers and mushroom gatherers sometimes rested there. But it was no place for someone alone at night.

The stepmother nagged and nagged. What could the father do? Luba herself finally wanted to go, just to give her father some peace.

Two such shrewish women were just too much for the father and his gentle daughter!

So the father at last obeyed the woman and took his daughter to the sod hut. He gave her a flint and steel, some work to do, and a sack of buckwheat.

Before he left he said to her, "Here is what you need for a fire. Don't let the fire go out. Boil some cereal and sit and spin. You must not leave the hut."

Night came. The girl heated up the stove and began boiling the buckwheat.

Suddenly — no one could say from where — a mouse raised its tiny voice and spoke to Luba. "Maiden, fair little maiden, give me a spoonful of porridge."

Now the girl was tired and bored from so much spinning. She was quite happy to see the mouse.

"Oh, little mouse, you bright-eyed creature!" she cried. "Just cheer me up a little and I will give you not one spoonful of porridge, but I will feed you good and full. Just take what you want."

So the mouse sang her a song:

"A bear went visiting out at the farm
With piles of honeycombs clutched in his arm,
Singing 'Yum yum yum and fiddle dum dee
The mouse should marry the humble bee!'
Sing along bear, dance along mouse —
We'll have a wedding in the forest house."

Then the mouse took a seat on the edge of the porridge pot and Luba fed him with the tip of her spoon just as she had promised. When the mouse went away, everything was quiet again.

But suddenly there was a shuffling and scraping

at the door. Then the door burst open and a bear came into the hut.

"Come on, little lady!" said the bear. "How about it? Are you ready? Put out the fire and let's play blindman's buff."

Luba had often played this game in her own cottage. A girl or boy would ring a little bell in the dark and then try to get away before the "blindman" could catch him. But whoever had played with a bear? Not Luba!

But to Luba's relief, the mouse came back, ran up on her shoulder, and whispered in her ear, "Don't be afraid, dear maiden! Say 'Ready, set, go!' Then put out the fire and slide under the stove. I'll do the running and I'll ring the little bell."

And so they played the game. The mouse rang the bell and the bear started after him — but he couldn't catch him!

Then the mouse rang from another corner and —whoosh!—the bear turned to grab him but missed.

The big bear waved his shaggy paws in the air, but the mouse was down on the floor. When the bear groped low, the mouse was up on the stove.

The bear became very angry. He was not used to losing. He was so angry he began throwing sticks of kindling wood and even logs around the room.

Finally the bear got tired of throwing sticks

and said, "Little lady, you are an expert at playing blindman's buff! And just for that, tomorrow I'll send you a drove of horses pulling a wagon full of presents."

And with that the bear left the hut.

Luba crawled out from under the stove and went to sleep. The mouse settled in the crook of her arm.

The following day the stepmother said to her husband, "Go along, old man, and check up on your daughter."

The stepmother was hoping something bad had happened during the night, but she said only, "See if Luba has finally done any spinning for us."

So the father drove off, and the stepmother sat down and waited for him to bring back the girl's bones.

Before long the dog came running from the forest. "Woof, woof, woof!" he barked. "Here comes the old man with his daughter. They're riding behind a drove of horses in a wagon full of honey and berries."

"You're lying, you mangy hound!" shouted the stepmother. "What you hear are the girl's bones rattling in a basket."

But in an instant the gates were squeaking, and into the yard ran the horses, with the daughter sitting next to her father in the wagon full of goods! Baskets of honey rocked in the rolling cart. Piles of berries glowed red and black like little velvet caps.

The stepmother's eyes burned with greed and envy. "What kind of impudence is this?" she screamed. "Turn right around and take my daughter Nastya into the forest for the night. She will come back with two droves of horses and two wagons full of goods."

The father obeyed and took Nastya to the forest. He was content to let the girl try her luck. He gave her the same supplies of flint and steel, buckwheat, and spinning flax.

To his stepdaughter he spoke the same bit of fatherly advice: "Here is what you need for a fire. Don't let the fire go out. Boil some cereal and sit and spin. You must not leave the hut."

Toward evening Nastya cooked up a pot of porridge. The mouse came into the hut and asked for some of it. Nastya was not generous like Luba. What an answer he got this time!

Nastya shrieked at him, "Get away, you piece of filth!" She threw the spoon at him and the mouse ran away. Nastya ate up all the porridge herself, blew out the fire, and settled down in a corner.

When it was deep night, the bear arrived at the forest hut. He knocked down the door and called,

"Hey, little lady, where are you? Let's play blind-man's buff."

Nastya kept silent, but she was so frightened her teeth chattered.

"There you are," called the bear. "Take the bell and run. I'll do the catching."

Nastya was so foolish she took the bell. But her hand was trembling and the bell rang wherever she went.

"Oh, oh!" said the mouse. "Now the bad-tempered girl is indeed done for."

The following day the stepmother got up early and sent her husband into the woods. "Get going there!" she told him. "Bring Nastya home. My daughter will bring back twice as much as Luba brought."

The father went to bring Nastya back from the hut in the forest. The stepmother waited in the yard.

Soon the dog came back. "Woof! Woof! Woof!" he barked. "Bones are rattling in the empty cart. The old man is sitting alone!"

"You're lying, you mongrel!" shouted the step-mother, and she gave him a kick. "My daughter is bringing back horses and goods."

But what the dog had said was true. When the stepmother saw her daughter's bones, she roared and shrieked and stamped on the ground.

It wasn't because of sorrow for her daughter, either — it was more from spite and jealousy. She was so angry she took sick and died the next day.

But the father and his daughter Luba lived out their days in peace. A fine son-in-law made the father's happiness complete.

The mouse never married the humble bee,
But the bear found more honey in an old oak tree.

A Red, Ripe Apple, A Golden Saucer

THERE ONCE LIVED IN A COSSACK VILLAGE AN OLD
man with his wife. They had three daughters. Two
of the girls were clever, but the third one, Tanya,
was nicknamed Little Fool. She was not really a fool,
though, just very quiet. She had good manners and
did not always try to get her own way.

The old man was a fisherman. Once when he
caught a lot of fish he decided to ride into town to
buy things.

The two clever daughters begged, "Father dear,
buy each of us a silken sarafan." A sarafan was a kind
of full coat, worn over a long dress.

"All right, I'll buy them," said the old man.

Little Fool didn't ask for anything. So her father
went up to her and said, "Tanya, little daughter,
why aren't you asking for anything? What should I
buy for you?"

"Nothing, Father dear. I don't need anything."

"But don't you want something? Some little present? Your sisters want me to buy silken sarafans. You can ask for something, too."

Tanya thought a minute and then asked, "Dear Father, buy me a red, ripe apple and a golden saucer."

Now apples could be bought at the market from peasants who raised fruit trees and lived by farming. So a red, ripe apple was no trouble at all.

But the old man was surprised when Tanya asked for a saucer. His family, like other Cossack families in their village, ate from wooden bowls carved at home. What could Tanya do with one china saucer painted gold? And what did it have to do with the apple? But it was really no trouble to buy such a saucer, either.

The old man finished his tasks and rode into town. When he got there, he went to the bazaar and bought each of the older daughters a silken sarafan. For the youngest he bought a red, ripe apple and a golden saucer. He had presents for everyone then, and he started home.

When the fisherman got back to the village, he took the presents in to his daughters. The older, clever daughters combed their hair, put on the sarafans, and went out to take a walk.

But the youngest daughter stayed at home. She

combed her hair, put on a nice skirt, and sat down.
Then she put the golden saucer on her knees. On top
of it she put the red, ripe apple. Then she started
talking:

> "Sliding, sliding little saucer,
> Gliding, gliding little apple,
> Let me see wide fields, vast seas,
> Broad meadows, tall trees,
> Hunter's bow, flying arrow,
> Lovely mountains high
> Reaching to the sky."

As soon as she spoke something wonderful happened. A beautiful countryside appeared before her,
with mountains by the sea and hunters riding far,
far up along the mountainside into castles of clouds.

When the older daughters got back from their
walk and saw what Tanya's apple and saucer could
do, sure enough, they began to be envious. So they
said, "Dear sister, sweet little Tanya, let us play a
while with the red, ripe apple and the golden
saucer."

"Go ahead and play," Tanya answered.

The sisters took Tanya's presents and began to
play with them. The older girl said,

> "Sliding, sliding little saucer,
> Gliding, gliding little apple,
> Let me see wide fields, vast seas,

Broad meadows, tall trees,
Hunter's bow, flying arrow,
Lovely mountains high
Reaching to the sky."

And once again the beautiful scene appeared.

The older sisters liked Tanya's red, ripe apple and golden saucer much better than their own silken sarafans. So they began begging, trying to get Tanya to give up her gifts.

"Give them to us, dear little sister. Give us the red, ripe apple and golden saucer. Sweet Tanya! We will give you our silken sarafans."

"No, dear sisters, I can't do that," the girl answered. "The red, ripe apple and golden saucer were gifts from Father. He asked me what I wanted and then found them in the market. If I give my presents to you, he'll think I didn't like them. But why not ask Father yourselves? Maybe he will buy the same for you. But I don't need the silken sarafans."

The older sisters were very angry at the youngest. But they hid their feelings and didn't say anything.

Some time passed. Tanya forgot her conversation with her sisters, but she liked her apple and saucer so much that she kept them with her always.

Then one day the older sisters asked Little Fool to go with them into the forest.

"Come with us to the woods for strawberries," they begged. "It's more fun if we all three go."

"All right," answered Tanya. "If you want, I'll go."

So she went with them, never suspecting her sisters meant her harm. The three girls walked along until they came into the dense woods.

Suddenly the older sisters turned upon Tanya. They seized her and killed her and buried her beneath a tree. Then they took the red, ripe apple and the golden saucer for themselves.

In the evening, the older sisters returned from the woods. They had already agreed on what to tell their father.

"Oh, Father!" they cried. "Our Little Fool went away somewhere. We searched and searched, shouted and shouted, but we didn't find her. We looked everywhere until it got dark." Then they pretended to cry.

"Wherever can she have gone?" asked the father.

"We don't know," said the two girls. "Maybe the goblins got her."

But the father loved his youngest daughter because she was always so affectionate and kind. He wept many real tears for Tanya.

He didn't really believe his older daughters when they said their little sister had gotten lost. And

he couldn't believe that the loving child was dead and gone from the world.

For a whole week the father wept and waited for little Tanya to come back. He wept a second week, then a third week, but still he couldn't believe his Tanya was dead, even though she did not return.

"Probably those envious girls led her deep into the woods and abandoned her there," he thought to himself.

In this Cossack village was a shepherd. He was a young man chosen by the villagers to take the sheep out to graze. He watched the sheep wherever they went so they would not stray and get lost.

One day, the shepherd took his herd into the woods where the sisters had led Tanya. He drove the sheep on and on, and finally came upon a little mound in the woods. Atop that mound a slender reed had grown. He sat down on the mound to rest. He had no idea it was the place where Tanya had been buried.

He got out a knife, thinking, "I'll cut off the reed and make myself a pipe. Then I'll play a tune on it."

He cut off the slender reed, made a pipe, and got ready to play. But when he played on the pipe, the pipe spoke to him:

"Three sisters were we, sisters three,

We went to the woods for the berries so red,
So red the berries, berries so red.
My sisters have killed me,
My sisters have stilled me,
The dark earth has chilled me —
For the red, ripe apple,
For the golden saucer."

The shepherd was amazed. A talking reed! He thought he was just imagining it. So he decided to play again.

He blew on his reed pipe, and the pipe spoke to him once more with the same sad song. It spoke in a maiden's gentle voice, sounding as if it were crying for something lost.

Evening came. The shepherd drove the herd of sheep back into the Cossack village. As he walked along the path, he played on the pipe. Again the pipe spoke in a maiden's gentle voice. The voice was Tanya's, and it repeated the same sad story.

The path took the shepherd past the old fisherman's house. When Tanya's father heard the words, he rushed out to the shepherd and cried, "Give me the pipe!"

The shepherd handed the reed pipe to the old man. The father did not know how to play, but the pipe just started out on its own:

"My own dearest mother,

My own dearest father,

We went to the woods for the berries so red,

So red the berries, berries so red . . ."

Right away the old man understood and began to cry bitterly. Then he asked the shepherd where he had found the pipe. The shepherd told him how he had found the reed growing on a little mound and how the magical pipe told a story of its own.

Then the fisherman went into the woods himself. He found the mound of earth where the shepherd said the reed had grown. When the old man dug up the ground, he saw his own Tanya lying there, appearing as if alive.

He took his daughter into his arms, but she was dead. Mournfully, he carried the girl home.

On the way, the fisherman stopped in the village to see an old woman who knew something about magic. He asked for her help.

"Go to the Tsar," the old woman said. "Take some water from his well. Sprinkle your daughter with that water and she will come to life."

The older sisters, the evildoers, began to shriek when they saw their father carrying home the sister they had killed. They cried and howled and tore their hair. They were terrified at what their father might do now.

But the fisherman had no time for them. He

rode straight to the Tsar to get water from his well.

The Tsar saw the old Cossack and asked, "What do you need the water for?"

The old man told the Tsar everything. The Tsar was so moved by the fisherman's story that he gave him the water himself.

"If the maiden awakens," the Tsar said, "bring her to me and have her bring her treasure with her."

The father rode home and sprinkled the water on his daughter. After a minute she stood up. The fisherman was so happy that he forgot to punish the older sisters. He took Tanya and the red, ripe apple and the golden saucer and went to the Tsar.

As soon as the Tsar looked at Tanya he fell in love with her. The Tsar had her play with the red, ripe apple and golden saucer. Tanya took the red, ripe apple and golden saucer and said:

"Sliding, sliding little saucer,
Gliding, gliding little apple,
Reveal to me wide fields, vast seas,
Broad meadows, tall trees,
Hunter's bow, flying arrow,
Lovely mountains high
Reaching to the sky."

The lovely countryside appeared again as soon as Tanya spoke the words.

Then the Tsar said to himself, "I should take

a girl like that as my wife." He thought it over for a while and then asked the fisherman's daughter, "Will you marry me?"

"I will," answered Tanya. Then she added, "Only, dear Father, sovereign Tsar, let my sisters live with me. I am sorry for them. Don't punish them. Let them live with us."

"Let it be so," said the Tsar.

The Tsar and Tanya were married, and the Tsar found that Tanya was affectionate, beautiful, gentle, and well-mannered, too.

The two sisters were envious of Tanya, but they could do nothing about it. So while the fisherman's little daughter lived happily with the Tsar, the jealous sisters began to make mischief to vent their anger.

Things went on this way for a long time. The Tsar was not blind. He kept a careful watch on the sisters. At first he was patient. Then he was patient some more. Finally, however, he had to drive them away from his realm and he felt at ease.

Now everyone led a happy life. The Tsar and Tanya lived together for a long time, enjoying what they had. The red, ripe apple never withered, and the golden saucer was never broken.

Alyosha Popovich

ONE NIGHT, WHEN THE BRIGHT MOON WAS BORN IN heaven a son was born on earth to the old sexton of a church. This sexton was a priest named Leonty.

A son was born — but not just any son. No! He was a warrior. They called him Alyosha Popovich, which means "Alyosha the priest's son." It was a fine name for a fine youngster.

Alyosha was given as much as he wanted to eat and drink from the very start. And how he grew! You could tell he was a warrior and not just an ordinary baby. He grew in a day as much as someone else would grow in a week. What someone else could do in a year, he could polish off in only a month.

Before long, Alyosha went to school. He learned his lessons well, but he was very independent. When the others said "Black," he said "White."

When they said "Left," he said "Right." When they said "Go over there," he said "Come over here and get me." But he always spoke politely.

He tried playing with the other children. He was gentle, but he was just too strong for them. If Alyosha grabbed someone by the leg — off it came! If he grabbed someone by the arm — that was the end of the arm. If he held someone by the middle — good-bye stomach! He thought his games were fun, but it wasn't easy to find playmates.

In a while Alyosha was grown up. He learned from his father how to pray and how to ride a horse alone out on the open steppe. His mother taught him to behave and to speak in a nice way.

At last Alyosha was ready to leave home. His father said, "Since you're on your own now, take along someone who can keep you company and do what you do. Why not take faithful Maryshko, Paranov's son?"

"All right," said Alyosha.

"And mind your manners," said his mother, giving him a pie for the trip.

So the two young men got up on good horses. They rode off through the open steppe so fast that clouds of dust rose like pillars in the sky. The trees and the clouds were blotted out and you couldn't see anything but the trail of the two riders.

The two of them rode to Prince Vladimir. Alyosha Popovich went straight into the bright stone palace, right up to the prince. He made the sign of the cross like a deacon. He bowed to the four corners of the earth just like a learned man. Then he bowed to Prince Vladimir personally.

Vladimir greeted the good companions and gave them a seat at the oak table. He brought out plenty to eat, gave them drink, and sat with them hoping for a bit of news.

The young friends began to eat stacks and stacks of honey cakes. A whole barrel of strong wine went down after the cakes. When he saw how much they were eating, Prince Vladimir got worried.

"Who are you, you good fellows?" he asked. "Are you warriors, strong and ready to help a prince in trouble? Or are you just wanderers, passing through? What did you bring with you? Sharp swords to fight or empty saddlebags to stuff with my honey cakes? By the way, I don't know your names or your fathers' names either."

Alyosha answered, "I am Alyosha Popovich, the son of Leonty the priest, the old sexton at the village church. My friend is Maryshko, son of Paranov."

"Did you bring anything for me?" asked Vladimir hopefully.

"No," said Alyosha. "You already have everything."

Then he added politely, "But my sword is
ready to serve you. First, though, I need a rest
after that meal. Thank you very much for such
good food and wine." And Alyosha started getting
settled on the brick stove.

The prince's stove was not just a stove for
cooking. It was more like a big baking oven with a
flat brick top as wide as a table. It was used to keep
the palace warm in winter. Every hut in Alyosha's
village had a stove like that, but not as big or as
wide as the prince's. The stove was the best place
for a nap because it was so warm. Alyosha scratched
himself on all sides and lay down for a little sleep.
Maryshko stayed sitting at the table.

At that time — it was years and years ago — the
kingdom had a terrible enemy. The trouble was
caused by Tugarin, a dragon's son. He kept invad-
ing Vladimir's lands, flying all around and breath-
ing fire.

Tugarin was not afraid of royalty. He would
come right into the bright stone palace without
asking. First he would blow open the door. Then,
with a loud stamp, he would put one foot on the
threshold and plant another foot on the oak table.
The rest of his feet would settle on benches along

the wall. Then he would start eating and drinking. Every so often he would steal away a princess when he left the table, and then bring her back when he got hungry again.

And Tugarin made a real joke of Prince Vladimir! Whenever Tugarin came, the prince would duck down very quietly behind the stove, trying to escape notice. Tugarin would scold him and send puffs of hot air into the prince's hiding place.

"I do wish," thought Prince Vladimir to himself, "that someone would get rid of that Tugarin. It isn't as nice being a prince as it used to be."

But the biggest problem was Tugarin's eating. That dragon would put a roast goose on the back of his tongue, pile cakes between his teeth, snatch up a pie with his front fangs, and swallow everything down in one gulp. When he drank the prince's strong wine or had some beer, the barrels went down, too. He chewed up the silver and gold cups. One day, when there wasn't enough regular food, Tugarin began eating the table. Then he used the broom as a toothpick.

Now on this day, as Alyosha Popovich was lying on the brick stove, Tugarin came by the palace for a visit. Alyosha was disgusted by the dragon's manners, so he gave him a lecture.

"My old father, the priest Leonty, had a fat cow

— a big fat glutton. This cow would go around to all the beer breweries and drink up whole barrels of beer. She even took the lees at the bottom. Then this cow, this big fat glutton, went to the lake and started drinking all the water out of it. Was that right? Was that polite? So one day we grabbed her and pounded her flat. We turned her into a beef-steak! And that, Tugarin, is the way we'll yank *you* out from behind the table and teach you to be polite to the brave Prince Vladimir."

Tugarin stopped chewing out of sheer amaze-ment. No one had dared to speak to him like that before. The dragon lost his temper. He flew into a terrible fury against Alyosha Popovich. He threw a fine knife at him and tried to blow him off the stove and step on him.

But Alyosha Popovich was light on his feet. He slipped behind an oak post when the knife was thrown. Twang! went the knife into the wood. Alyosha smiled and made a polite little speech.

"Thank you very kindly, Tugarin, son of a dragon, for giving me this fine, well-tempered knife. You must be a warrior to have such a weapon. I will make good use of it to slice open your white belly. Your bright eyes will be darkened and I'll just have a look at your daring heart."

Maryshko, Paranov's son, wanted to get in on

the fun, too. He jumped up from the table and grabbed Tugarin by the scruff of the neck. He snatched him out from behind the table and threw him against the palace wall. All the latticed windows came crashing down in little pieces.

Alyosha yawned and got up on the stove again. "Oh, Maryshko!" he sighed in admiration, "Maryshko, Paranov's son, you are a faithful friend, faithful and true!"

Maryshko replied, "Just give me the well-tempered knife a minute, will you, Alyosha? I'll slice open Tugarin's belly. His bright eyes will be darkened and I'll just take a look at his daring heart."

Alyosha answered, "Oh, Maryshko! You brave warrior! If you go and do that, you'll wreck the palace. Look at how we've already broken those fine windows teaching Tugarin his place. Better let him out into the open steppe — he can't go too far. Tomorrow morning we will meet him out in the open, in the fields."

So Tugarin was allowed to leave the palace.

The next morning, very early, Maryshko rose with the sun and led the spirited horses to drink at a swift river.

Tugarin the dragon's son came up to Maryshko and asked him to invite Alyosha Popovich out into the field. He even tried to be polite. "Be so kind," he said, "as to ask Alyosha the priest's son to come out here. He has my knife — the dog! — and I want very much to say hello to him."

Maryshko rode back to the palace to wake Alyosha.

"God is your judge, Alyosha Popovich! You didn't give me the well-tempered knife. Then I could have finished that dragon off yesterday. But now you see? What can you expect from that Tugarin? He's flying way up in the heavens now. You can't reach him up there."

"I suppose I have to get up and handle this myself," said Alyosha. "Otherwise whatever happens will be my fault. I'm the one who took Tugarin's knife from him."

Alyosha led out his good horse, put a bright leather saddle on him, and fastened it with twelve silken saddle girths. He rode out into the field, but not for his own glory. He was trying to save the palace from that dragon Tugarin.

Alyosha rode out alone and saw Tugarin flying up in the heavens. He was in a bad spot because he could be attacked from above. But he remembered his father's lessons and began to pray: "Most Holy Mother of God! Order up a big black cloud, will you? Have the cloud pour out a heavy rain with big drops. Maybe the drops will wash the paper wings off Tugarin. Then I can slay him."

Alyosha's prayer worked. A black cloud came rolling up. Then a heavy rain came down. The big drops washed the wings right off the dragon. He fell down with a thud to the damp ground. Now Tugarin, like any other warrior, had to walk to meet Alyosha in the open field.

When Tugarin and Alyosha met in battle you might have thought two mountains were crashing together. They struck with war clubs — the clubs split down the middle. They hit each other with lances — the lances split into shivers. They slashed with swords — the swords became dented and dull.

Suddenly Alyosha Popovich fell from his saddle like a sheaf of oats. There was Tugarin, ready to pound him flat.

Was that to be the end of Leonty's son? Not at all!

Alyosha was quick footed and quick thinking. He rolled away under his horse and stood up on the other side. Then he jumped from behind his horse and struck Tugarin under his right shoulder with the well-tempered knife.

Tugarin fell and Alyosha looked down at the beast. He had been a brave warrior, even if he had been a glutton.

"Thank you very kindly, Tugarin the dragon's

son, for the well-tempered knife," said Alyosha.
"I'll keep it in your honor." And saying this, he
struck off the dragon's head.

Alyosha decided to bring back the fierce head
to show the prince that he had kept his word. He
rode along on his horse holding his prize high on
his spear.

Prince Vladimir was watching out the window. He saw the dragon's head up high and Alyosha's head down below. He nearly fainted on the
spot. Then he started to cry.

"Look!" the prince said. "Tugarin is bringing
back the head of Alyosha Popovich! Now Tugarin
will take our whole kingdom into captivity! What's
the use of being prince then?"

Maryshko looked at the prince crouching under
the table. He raised his sword and made an encour-
aging speech. "Don't cry, Vladimir, Crimson Sun,
Chief Warrior, Bravest of the Brave, noble Prince
of Kiev! If Tugarin is coming close to the earth
and not flying through the sky, then I'll make him
bend his head to my spear. Don't pout, Prince.
Come out from under there and watch how I go
out and say hello to Tugarin!"

Then Maryshko looked out the window. Alyosha was still far off, so Maryshko borrowed the
prince's telescope. As soon as he looked through it,

he saw that his friend Alyosha Popovich was the victor.

"I see a brave warrior riding toward the palace!" Maryshko announced. "A young champion with a proud step. Alyosha is rearing up on his horse, tossing the dragon's head high in the air and catching it on his spear. Cheer up, Prince! It isn't Tugarin the pagan who is coming, but Alyosha Popovich, son of Leonty the old sexton! And he's bringing the head of Tugarin the dragon's son with him!"

Thus did a poor boy save a kingdom. Prince Vladimir ordered a great feast, and the merrymaking went on for days.

Vasilisa and Prince Vladimir

THIS HAPPENED WHEN VLADIMIR WAS PRINCE OF Kiev.

Prince Vladimir was feasting and celebrating with his warriors, envoys from other princes, and merchants from trading cities. Everyone was eating and drinking as much as he wanted.

While the feasting was going on, the guests started to boast about the different things they had done. All the guests were proud men, but the warriors talked the loudest and bragged about what they had done in battle and in private quarrels.

One guest was from Chernigov. He was a merchant named Stavr Rodionovich. He heard the bragging, but he sat at the table without smiling. He did not drink the foaming wine or eat the goose stuffed with nuts. Prince Vladimir noticed this and came over to speak to him.

"Why aren't you eating and drinking, Stavr Rodionovich?" the prince asked. "Why, you're sitting here without even a smile! You haven't told us about your brave and great deeds. Well . . . it is true that you don't come from a famous family. And since you're not a warrior, but a merchant, you're not known for brave fighting. A merchant is just a merchant—I suppose you really don't have anything to boast about at all."

"What you say is true, great prince," Stavr answered. "I don't have anything to boast about. I am just a merchant, as you say. My father and mother died long ago, or I would praise them. I don't feel like talking about all the gold in my treasury—I don't even know myself how much I have. I could spend my whole life counting it, and I wouldn't be finished when I died.

"Why boast about fine clothes the way your courtiers do?" Stavr continued. "You're all wearing my clothes to this feast. I have forty tailors working day and night for me. Why, sometimes I wear a new coat for a day, then I just sell it to you. The next day I wear another one.

"Where would you get your weapons if it weren't for my merchant ships?" Stavr asked. "Why, my horses are golden maned and my sheep have a golden fleece. I sell these creatures to you, too.

You are glad to buy my goods even though I am just a merchant.

"But wait! Listen to this," he went on. "I'll just boast a little about my wife Vasilisa, the eldest daughter of Mikulisha Selyanin. There isn't another girl like her in the world. Her red braids are so glossy the moon shines from them. Her eyebrows are blacker than sable. Her eyes are brighter than a falcon's. There isn't a smarter person in all Russia. And as for you, Prince, well, she would wind you all around her little finger and you would lose your head over her, even though you think you have everything a man could want."

Everyone at the feast was afraid. What a daring way to talk! It was dangerous to insult the prince like that. The guests sat and looked at Stavr. All talking stopped and it was silent in the palace at Kiev.

The Princess Apraksia, Vladimir's wife, felt insulted, too. She began to cry. Could Stavr's wife really take the prince away from her? What if it were true?

Prince Vladimir shook with rage. His loud voice filled the whole palace as he spoke.

"Faithful servants, come here and seize Stavr! Drag him down into the cold dungeon and fasten him to the stone wall with iron chains. That's what he gets for his insulting way of talk! He'll have well water to drink and raw oats to eat. Let him sit in the dungeon until he comes to his senses. We'll just see how smart his wife really is. How she turns all our heads! And how she gets Stavr out of prison!"

But Prince Vladimir wasn't satisfied with just putting Stavr in the cold, damp dungeon. He ordered a guard to the city of Chernigov to put the prince's own seal on all of Stavr Rodionovich's wealth and to bring his wife back to Kiev in chains.

"We'll just see whether she really is so clever," the prince said.

In the meantime, while the prince's men were getting ready to leave, putting on their weapons, shoeing the horses and saddling them, news of what had happened to Stavr reached Vasilisa in the city of Chernigov.

Vasilisa cried and cried. She had lost her dear husband. She wept for a while all alone. Then suddenly she shook her head, straightened up, and started thinking.

"There's not much sense in crying," she said to herself. "I have to do something. The prince won't take money for my dear Stavr. And I can't take him away by force either. We have our own guards, but the prince has a thousand men. All right," she thought, "since I can't get him by force, I'll get him

by strategy. I'll use my wits to free him."

Then Vasilisa went out into the entranceway. She called her serving girls to her in a firm voice. They were all beautiful maidens, but not as lovely as Vasilisa.

"Come here, my faithful girls, all of you! Now do what I ask you to do. I will go to Kiev to rescue by dear husband."

The girls were frightened when they heard that. Could their mistress dare oppose the prince?

"Saddle the best horse for me," Vasilisa went on, "and bring me men's clothes, the kind Tatars wear, not Russian things. Cut off my braids. I'm riding straight to Prince Vladimir."

At that time there were great troubles in the Russian land. Only a few years before, some of the largest Russian cities had fallen into captivity. The invaders were Tatars who came sweeping across the steppe from the East. Their leader was the Khan. The Khan's soldiers and nobles were called the Golden Horde.

The Tatars attacked the Russian cities, but they did not always stay to rule once they had conquered them. Instead, they forced the Russian ruler to recognize the Khan as his lord and to send a tribute to the Golden Horde once a year. The tribute had to be paid in money or men.

It was hard on the princes. If the Russians didn't pay what the Tatars demanded, the Golden Horde would again send out soldiers to destroy the city and the countryside. Some cities in the north of Russia were still free. But Kiev, in the south, had had to bow to the Golden Horde.

Vasilisa's plan was to dress as a Tatar. If she came to Kiev as just another Russian, no one would pay much attention to her. But as an envoy of the Golden Horde, she would command respect.

The serving girls brought in the clothes and Vasilisa dressed. When the girls saw her, they began to cry again. Vasilisa looked so strange in the Tatar clothes.

Then it was time to cut off Vasilisa's red braids. Soon her long hair covered the floor. It was so bright the moon seemed to shine from it.

Vasilisa gathered together some weapons and some soldiers. She put a bow and arrows on her back, mounted her horse, and galloped with her men toward the city of Kiev. No one would have believed this magnificent soldier was a woman.

Vasilisa was riding through the fields like a regular warrior when Prince Vladimir's men met her halfway. "Hey there, soldier!" they shouted. "Where are you headed?"

"I'm riding to Prince Vladimir as an envoy

from the Golden Horde. I'm ordered to bring back twelve years' worth of tribute. And what about you men? Where are you heading?"

"We're going to Chernigov to find Vasilisa Mikulisha. We're going to take her in chains to Kiev and bring her wealth to the prince."

"You're too late, brothers," Vasilisa replied. "Her own guard carried off the money when they heard how angry the prince was. And I sent Vasilisa to the Golden Horde."

The prince's men talked things over. "Well, if that's the way it is," they said among themselves, "then there's nothing for us to do in Chernigov. We'll go back to Kiev."

The prince's soldiers sent messengers ahead to ride hard to the prince and tell him what had happened. The most important news was that an envoy was coming from the Golden Horde.

The prince was gloomy when he heard. "I can't scrape up twelve years' worth of tribute," he said.

But the prince managed to think up a plan with his wife Apraksia. They decided to play up to the envoy and win him over by being respectful and showing him hospitality. So they had the tables laid and spruce branches thrown down in the courtyard to honor him. They put lookouts on the walls to wait for his arrival.

But Vasilisa didn't ride into the city of Kiev with her men. She put up her tent in the fields and left her soldiers there. Then she rode in alone to the prince.

Everyone who saw her was fooled. No one suspected this was a woman. The Tatar envoy seemed good looking, but he was only fairly tall and strong. His face was not threatening. Maybe, the people thought, he would be easy to deal with. He was certainly respectful and knew all the ceremonies of the court.

Vasilisa rode up to the palace, jumped off her horse, and tied it to the golden porch. Then she went into the great hall and bowed low to the north and the south, the east and the west. Then she bowed to the prince individually, and to the princess, too. She bowed lowest of all to Zabava Putyashna, a lovely young niece of the prince.

Prince Vladimir then spoke to the envoy. "Welcome, mighty envoy from the Golden Horde. Take a seat at the place of honor. Rest a while. Eat and drink with us at our princely table after your long ride."

But the envoy was not persuaded by flattery. "There is no time for an envoy of the Golden Horde to sit and rest," said Vasilisa in a firm voice. "I am Vasilly, come from the Khan of the Horde. The

Khan does not ask for hospitality. He demands the tribute due him for twelve years. Be quick about getting it ready and take away your fine feasts and speeches."

Prince Vladimir was worried. Their plan did not seem to be working. But in another moment he became more hopeful.

"Give me that woman, Zabava, for a wife," said the envoy. "Then I will return to the Golden Horde."

The prince now saw a chance of winning over the envoy by letting him marry into his own family. But he had to talk with Zabava first.

"If you will permit, mighty envoy," said the prince, "I will just have a word with my niece."

The prince led Zabava aside and asked, "Zabava, will you go with the envoy of the Golden Horde? He speaks and acts nobly. Maybe you like him already. You were staring at him while he spoke to me."

Zabava leaned over and whispered into Prince Vladimir's ear. "What's gotten into your head, Uncle dear? Don't make us into a joke for the whole of Russia. Why, that isn't a warrior at all. That envoy is a woman!"

The prince was angry. "Your hair is long, but you're short on brains," he said. "That's an envoy of the Golden Horde. He is named Vasilly."

"He's not a warrior, he's a woman," Zabava insisted. "He walks through the hall like a swan floating on the water. His heels don't make a thumping sound on the floor. When he sits, he squeezes his knees together. He has a silvery voice, too, don't you hear? And small hands and feet, and slender fingers. Why, you can even see traces of rings on his fingers!"

The prince thought it over. "Maybe I'd better give him a test," he said. He called out his best troops — the five Pritchenkov brothers and the two young Xopilovs. These men were all skilled fighters in hand-to-hand struggle.

Then Prince Vladimir went to the envoy and asked him, "Honored guest, while my niece gets ready, wouldn't you like to share in some sport with these fighters? Maybe a little contest in the great courtyard would just help to stretch your muscles after a long trip."

"I'd be glad of it," answered the envoy. "I've loved fighting ever since I was a child. Especially wrestling."

They all went out into the great courtyard. Vasilisa went into the middle of the circle of men. She didn't wait to be attacked, but grabbed three of the fighters with one hand and three with the other and tossed them into a heap. She piled the seventh on top and then bumped all their heads together. All seven were lying flat on the ground in a minute and couldn't get up.

Prince Vladimir spat and went away. That stupid Zabava! No sense at all. Calling a fighter like that a woman! They hadn't seen an envoy like that in a long time.

Zabava didn't give in. "That envoy is a woman, not a warrior," she insisted. And she made Vladimir give way a little once again.

The prince decided to try the envoy at another test. He led out the twelve best marksmen in Kiev. Then he said, "Honored guest, wouldn't you like to try out your bow with these marksmen?"

"Why not?" answered Vasilisa. "I've been shooting with bow and arrows since I was a child."

The twelve marksmen came out and shot arrows into a tall oak. The oak teetered and rocked as if a whirlwind had passed through it.

Then Vasilisa the envoy took up her bow. She pulled back the bowstring. The silk string zinged and the fiery arrow flew up through the air and arched back toward the ground. The arrow lashed into the oak, and the oak flew apart into tiny chips!

When the arrow struck the tree, the stoutest warriors couldn't stay on their feet because of the shock. Even Vladimir swayed along with his men.

"Well, I'm sorry about the oak," said Vasilisa. "But I'm even sorrier about spoiling my tempered arrow. Now I won't find another like it anywhere in Russia."

Vladimir went back to his niece. But Zabava still insisted, "A woman and nothing else!"

"Well," thought the prince, "I'll investigate a little closer myself. Women in Russia don't play chess. I'll try out the envoy at that."

And Vladimir ordered his men to bring out the golden chess pieces. Then he said to the envoy, "Vasilly, wouldn't you care for a game of chess? But watch out! When I was little I used to beat all the other children in chess, and checkers, too."

"What shall we play for, Prince? What are the stakes?"

"You put up the twelve years' tribute," said Prince Vladimir, "and I'll put up the whole city of Kiev."

"Agreed," said Vasilisa. "Let's play."

They started moving the chess pieces around the board. Prince Vladimir was a good player. He had a strategy in mind. But Vasilisa made a good move, then another good move, and another. On the tenth move she cornered Vladimir's king. Check! And then in one more move it was checkmate. The servants came and took the chess pieces away quietly.

Vladimir was terribly depressed. "You've taken my city away from me," he said. "You've taken Kiev. And I'm as good as in your power, too. Go ahead, mighty envoy. Take my head."

"I don't need your head, Prince," said Vasilisa, "and I don't need Kiev either. Just give me your niece, Zabava Putyashna."

The prince cheered up. He was in good spirits now and didn't go to ask Zabava again. He just ordered the palace servants to get the wedding feast ready. They would feast for three days and then the ceremony would be performed in the Cathedral of St. Sophia. Maybe he would be able to do something about the tribute when Vasilly was his own nephew.

They celebrated for one day, then another, and then the third day's festivities began. The guests were having a wonderful time.

But the bridegroom and his bride weren't so cheerful. Zabava was determined she was right, but the prince paid no attention to her. Instead, he looked after the envoy.

"Vasilly!" he said. "Why aren't you happy? Maybe you don't like our way of feasting? What can I order for your pleasure?"

"I don't know, Prince, I just feel anxious for some reason. I don't feel really cheerful. Maybe something has happened at home. Perhaps some misfortune is waiting ahead for me. Call in the lute players, let them cheer me up. They will sing about the old days and maybe about our times, too. They might give us a hint of what will happen later on. I'll find out what's ahead for me."

The prince had the lute players called in. The musicians sat and sang, strumming their instruments. They did their best, but the envoy still wasn't pleased.

"Prince," Vasilisa said, "these aren't real lute players. They're not the best singers either. But my father told me that you have a merchant here from Chernigov, Stavr Rodionovich I think his name is. I've heard it said that he's a man who can really play and sing songs. These men here are more like wolves howling in the fields. I'd like to hear that Stavr."

What could Prince Vladimir do? If he let Stavr out, he might lose his grasp on him. But if he didn't let him out, he'd anger the envoy.

Vladimir remembered the tribute that wasn't collected and ready. He decided he didn't dare anger Vasilly, so he ordered his men to bring in Stavr.

What a terrible sight Stavr was! But Vasilisa could not betray her disguise by showing concern. She knew her poor husband was weak and could barely stand on his own two legs, let alone sing songs. He was worn out from hunger.

Vasilisa said to Vladimir, "You'd better sit him down and give him plenty to eat and drink."

So the prince ordered that done, too.

Then when Stavr had finished eating, the envoy-bridegroom slid out from behind the table, took Stavr by the arm, and sat down next to him, asking Stavr to play something happy and to sing a while.

Stavr tuned his lute. Then he began to play and sing the songs of Chernigov.

All the guests at the tables stopped what they were doing and listened to him. His voice was weak from prison, but it was beautiful.

Vasilisa sat there, without taking her eyes off Stavr for even a minute. When Stavr had finished his songs, the envoy spoke to Vladimir. "Listen, Prince Vladimir of Kiev. Give me this Stavr and I will forget about the tribute money and go back to the Golden Horde without it."

Prince Vladimir was not anxious to give Stavr up, but what could he do? The mighty Tatar envoy had asked. He would soon be marrying Vladimir's own niece, too, so how could he refuse?

The prince said, "Take him, Vasilly. You are as good as a part of my family now." He paused and said, "The wedding is tomorrow. Will you return to the Golden Horde after that?"

In truth, Vladimir was sad at the thought that

Vasilly would soon be leaving. The prince was strangely attracted to the young, handsome envoy with the bright eyes, though he couldn't say why.

That evening, Vasilisa didn't wait for the end of the feast. She agreed with Prince Vladimir that she would take Stavr back to her tent and keep him there.

"You go on feasting. I'll soon be back," said Vasilisa to Zabava. And the envoy jumped on his horse, put Stavr behind, and galloped out toward the tent.

The envoy asked Stavr, "Don't you recognize me, Stavr Rodionovich? We learned our alphabet together."

"I've never seen you before, envoy of the Tatars," replied Stavr. His face was dark and sad, for he believed he had exchanged Vladimir's dungeon for captivity in the Tatar camp.

"Yes, you have," continued Vasilisa. "When we were little I used to follow you about and watch you learn to use a bow and arrow. I even tried a few shots myself. And I know all your tricks in fighting, too."

Stavr was puzzled and didn't know what to say.

When they reached the envoy's encampment, Vasilisa slipped into the tent leaving Stavr at the entrance. Quickly she threw off her man's clothes and put on a woman's dress. She arranged her hair and came out.

"Hello, dear Stavr!" she said. "You boasted about your young wife, about how she was so smart and brave and beautiful. And she really did wind everyone around her little finger. Don't you recognize her now either?"

Stavr looked. Then he looked again. He could hardly believe his eyes. Was this the warrior who had boldly ordered the prince to open the prison and let him out? Stavr put his arms around Vasilisa and drew her close to him. Then he kissed her hands.

"My beloved wife, you clever girl, Vasilisa," he cried. "Thank you for saving me from prison!" Then he stood back and looked at her again. "But where are your red braids?"

"Dearest husband! I used those braids to draw you up out of the dungeon, out of that deep pit."

Stavr bowed low to his wife. He thanked her from his heart and loved her even more for what she had done.

Vasilisa laughed happily. "It's a good thing you play chess with me at home," she said. "I really beat the prince."

Stavr hugged her again and then said, "Let's mount the fastest horses we have and ride away to Chernigov."

"It's dishonorable, Stavr, to run away in secret," Vasilisa replied. "You would never do such a thing, but you are worried about me. No, let's go back together to the palace and finish off the feast."

So they put on their richest clothes and ornaments and returned to Kiev. They walked into the hall and up to the prince.

Vladimir was astonished. There was Stavr with his young wife! And she looked so familiar!

Vasilisa said to Vladimir, "Well, Prince Vladimir, Crimson Sun, I am the mighty envoy and I am Stavr's wife. I've come back for the wedding. After the feast comes the ceremony, you know. Will you still give me your niece for my wife?"

Zabava jumped up and cried, "I told you, Uncle, that you shouldn't make us a laughingstock of all Russia! You almost married a maiden to a woman!"

"Maybe you ought to take more notice of what women say," said Vasilisa. "They often notice things that escape a man's eye."

The prince hung his head in shame. And the warriors and boyars laughed until they nearly choked. All the guests praised Vasilisa. Then Vladimir shook his head and laughed a little himself. He stood up.

"What a woman!" he said in admiration. "Well,

Stavr Rodionovich, you were right to boast about your young wife. She is beautiful, and she wound us all around her little finger, too. And she even turned my head a little. Don't let anyone blame you for boasting about her. For your wife, and because of the harm I did you, I will give you the best presents from my treasure."

So Stavr Rodionovich and the lovely Vasilisa gathered their things up to go home to Chernigov. They received many presents, and the prince and princess themselves walked out to see them off. The warriors, the boyars, and the guests and servants did, too.

On the way to Chernigov Stavr took out his lute and made up songs praising Vasilisa. She sang with him about how much she loved her dear husband, and they both sang about the long red braids that had turned into a rope to pull Stavr from the deep dungeon of Kiev Palace.

After they got home, they lived together for years in love and agreement with one another. They already had a good supply of wealth and property. They matched it with a fine supply of strong children.

And even now people sing songs about Vasilisa, the wise woman, brave and beautiful, and they tell her story to all their children.